Red Unicorn

Don't get left behind!

STARSCAPE

Let the journey begin . . .

From the Two Rivers
The Eye of the World: Part One
by Robert Jordan

To the Blight
The Eye of the World: Part Two
by Robert Jordan

Ender's Game
by Orson Scott Card

The Cockatrice Boys
by Joan Aiken

Mairelon the Magician
by Patricia C. Wrede

The Whispering Mountain
by Joan Aiken

Ender's Shadow
by Orson Scott Card

The Garden Behind the Moon
by Howard Pyle

Orvis
by H. M. Hoover

The Dark Side of Nowhere
by Neal Shusterman

Prince Ombra
by Roderick MacLeish

The Magician's Ward
by Patricia C. Wrede

A College of Magics
by Caroline Stevermer

Pinocchio
by Carlo Collodi

Deep Secret
by Diana Wynne Jones

Another Heaven, Another Earth
by H. M. Hoover

Hidden Talents
by David Lubar

The Wonder Clock
by Howard Pyle

Obernewtyn
by Isobelle Carmody

The Shadow Guests
by Joan Aiken

This Time of Darkness
by H. M. Hoover

Song in the Silence
by Elizabeth Kerner

Putting Up Roots
by Charles Sheffield

Red Unicorn

TANITH LEE

A TOM DOHERTY ASSOCIATES BOOK
NEW YORK

RED UNICORN

Copyright © 1997 by Byron Preiss Visual Publications, Inc.
Text copyright © 1997 by Tanith Lee

A Starscape Book
Published by Tom Doherty Associates, LLC
175 Fifth Avenue
New York, NY 10010

www.starscapebooks.com

ISBN 0-765-34568-4

Summary: Feeling neglected because her sorceress mother is enamored with a flamboyant magician and her sister, Empress Lizra, is infatuated with her own true love, Tanaquil is drawn into another world in which her mirror self is plotting to murder her sister.

First Starscape Edition: April 2003

Printed in the United States of America

0   9   8   7   6   5   4   3   2   1

To the memory of my jade-eyed mother, Hylda Lee,
who first told me stories about witches,
princes, and magical beasts.

Foreword

(The story as told in *Book One: Black Unicorn* ...)

Sixteen-year-old Tanaquil, the red-haired daughter of red-haired sorceress Jaive, lives with her mother in a fortress in the desert. But Jaive's neglect, and her havoc-causing spells, make Tanaquil desperate to leave. She has some hopes of finding her father, although Jaive has never told her who he is. One night one of the peeves, desert animals who have begun to talk due to spillages of Jaive's magic, unearths the bones of a unicorn under the rock hills. Tanaquil has no apparent talent for magic, but she can mend things. She fixes the bones together. And presently the unicorn puts on flesh and comes alive. It leads Tanaquil—and the talking peeve—away into the desert.

Helped and hindered by the black unicorn, Tanaquil meets the Princess Lizra, in a city by the sea. And next, Lizra's father, the cold, difficult Prince Zorander, and his unpleasant counselor Gasb. The city has a legend of a fabulous unicorn which will bring a curse or a blessing. When the black unicorn appears it attacks the prince, whom

Tanaquil has by now discovered—to her disgust—is her father. Realizing the unicorn is the creature of another world, finer than her own, she locates the sorcerous gate-between-worlds in the cliffs by the sea. She mends it, and enables the unicorn to return. But the peeve follows the unicorn through, so Tanaquil must also follow.

The black unicorn's world is the Perfect World, every-thing is beautiful, balanced, peaceful, good. To her horror, finding her mere presence seems to injure this perfection, Tanaquil, with the peeve, goes back to her own world, mag-ically closing the gate behind her.

However, when Gasb attempts to have her killed, she learns that the unicorn has made both her and the peeve invulnerable. They are safe from all danger. She must face the fact that the peeve is her familiar, and, with her amaz-ing knack of mending, she is a sorceress.

Zorander is ill, and Tanaquil's sister, Lizra, declares she must stay with him. But Tanaquil sets out with the peeve to see her own world at last.

(The story as continued in *Book Two: Gold Unicorn* . . .)

After a year of travelling, Tanaquil is coming back towards Zorander's kingdom, to see her mother in the desert. There is talk of war, and on her way Tanaquil has an en-counter with the powerful, clever and irritating magician, Worabex. He has apparently made a weapon against the much-feared invading empress, Lizora Veriam. The weapon turns out to be some things called mousps, a cross between wasps and mice.

As Tanaquil rides on, she is arrested by soldiers of the wicked empress's army. But when she meets the empress, she is none other than Tanaquil's sister Lizra. Zorander is dead, and Lizra has taken on the rule of his kingdom— and much of his cold, unfortunate manner. She is also now obsessed with conquering the world and so making it 'better' with kindly helpful laws. Of course, no one wishes to be conquered, and it is war all the way.

Lizra's artisans have made a steam-driven unicorn plated with gold, which, marching before the army, will inspire terror and so make conquest easier. However, it will not go, so Tanaquil, more or less Lizra's prisoner, is unwillingly forced to mend it. Naturally her magic does the trick and the unicorn strides out, causing fear and damage. A story quickly grows that it is ill-fated to cross under the unicorn's belly. People who have done so have seemingly vanished.

As the war campaign drags on, Tanaquil comes to know Lizra's favourite, a young handsome mercenary captain called Honj. His men are called the Locusts. Lizra has made him a prince and he is obviously her love. Tanaquil and he can only argue whenever they meet, but the peeve likes him. Tanaquil is herself brought to grudgingly respect him, when she sees Honj is less self-serving than genuinely brave and compassionate.

Finally, having conquered yet one more city, Lizra's war camp is attacked by a large swarm of dangerously stinging mousps. In the confusion, Honj, Tanaquil and Lizra, the peeve, two of Honj's men and one non-stinging mousp, rush under the belly of the gold unicorn—and fall into another world.

Emblem of war that the unicorn is, the space beneath it has become a gate to a hell-world of red skies, black wastes, desolation and endless battle. They are joined by the others who have fallen into it, and set off on a grim trek. After witnessing an appalling skirmish, where *two* metal unicorns fight, they are surrounded by the bizarre forces of a demoniac war-lord, a creature with toothed eyes. He draws Lizra away to his palace to be his empress. To her companions' dismay she seems to go gladly. Revolted, Honj and his men, Spedbo and Mukk, can do little. Nor can Tanaquil, and after the peeve is abducted by an evil bird of black bone, she loses most of her spirit.

However, the peeve escapes, and in falling from the sky, manages to break Honj's arm. Tanaquil then discovers she can sorcerously mend bones also. She realizes that she loves Honj.

Lizra meanwhile outwits the emperor of hell, and gains a way for all of them to leave the hell-world. They see they have misjudged Lizra badly.

Once safely back into their own world of hopeful sunlight, Lizra calls a halt to her war of conquest. She is broken down and vulnerable after her experiences. Honj indicates to Tanaquil that he loves her as she loves him, but says he must stay with Lizra, who now needs him so badly. He asks Tanaquil for a silver ring she wears, and begs that she will go far away so as not to tempt him to break faith with Lizra. The general talk is that he will soon marry Lizra, and become her royal consort.

Bitterly sad, Tanaquil is at last returning to her mother's fortress, when Worabex makes a re-appearance. He tells Tanaquil he was the mousp who accompanied her into hell, and so knows all about everything. Now he wishes to visit her mother, Jaive, whom he has long admired from afar.

When Tanaquil angrily refuses his company, Worabex turns himself into a golden flea, and vanishes in the coat of the peeve. . . .

One

I

The first thing Tanaquil saw almost every morning on waking was the face of the man she loved. But that was because, for five or ten minutes at the start of each day, Tanaquil allowed herself to think about him. She pictured him, handsome, smiling, scowling, charming, unnerved, or simply blank. And once she had looked at him, with all her love and anger, she put him out of her mind. Or . . . she tried to.

Sometimes it was easy. At least for a few moments. As for example yesterday, when, on waking, she found a brown furry snout dangling a piece of cold limp toast, adrip with congealing melted cheese, an inch from her nose. "Uh, God, whatever? *Peeve!*"

The toast fell on her stomach.

The peeve stared at her hopefully.

"Nice? Hungry? Yes?"

"No. Revolting. *Not* hungry. For heaven's sake—"

At which the peeve scrambled down, and sitting on the

floor, gave itself a wash, starting with the bits of solidified cheese now stuck to its chest.

Tanaquil had sat up. She was contrite in a second, realizing the peeve had been trying to tempt her to eat.

"*Thank* you, anyway. It was very kind of you. It's just, first thing, I'd rather have something plainer, no, wait!"

Too late. The peeve had leaped out of the window. She sat in a faint uneasy despair, until it returned about half an hour after, and presented her with a completely unmoist, rather stale, slice of bread.

She ate some of this. It would have been too churlish not to. "Maybe a little butter would have . . . I don't know. This is probably best."

"Good," encouraged the peeve.

When she had eaten half the bread and drunk some water from her glass, the peeve climbed up and nuzzled into her arms.

She thought, desolately, *It knows I need to hold someone.*

She had only shed tears, in her sleep, once. She had dreamed of Honj, and that she had been going to meet him, under a tree in some flowery field. But when he rode up, he rode straight past her and away.

She ran three steps, and called his name, but no sound came from her throat, and all the grass and the flowers had grown much higher suddenly, and she could no longer see over them. Even if Honj had looked back, she would have been hidden.

That time the peeve had finally distracted her with gruesome antics on the floor. It pretended its tail was a dangerous snake, and—in order to stop the peeve from 'killing' its tail—Tanaquil had to leave her tears and her bed, and give it a slight shake.

Then it sprang to the window embrasure.

"Go out? Walks? Yes?"

"Maybe."

"Yes," decided the peeve, and dove out and over the roof of Tanaquil's mother's fortress in the desert. And for an instant, as she watched, Tanaquil remembered how she and it had first come together, in this very place, surrounded by the same glittering hot desert, under this dome of dry blue sky. But they had been different then. Even in memory, she could not really go back. Instead, always, she had to go forward. Out into some desert or other.

And the desert was in Tanaquil's mind now. Miles, miles of dunes and dust. But not a rock, not an oasis. No hope of any city.

This will have to stop.

Oh no, said the desert in her mind and heart. It never will.

When first she returned here, Tanaquil had thought she might be getting over her grief at losing Honj and her sister. She felt brighter with anger too, against Worabex. Convinced he lurked still in the peeve's fur as a golden flea, she had brushed and combed the peeve vigorously every day before breakfast and after supper, a process it had liked at the start, and then refused to put up with. At a small town, still some miles from the desert, there had been a fairly awful scene. Sheltering in a barn the peeve, rolling over and over and kicking to avoid Tanaquil's

Worabex-flea-searching comb, had cannoned into a small furnace, (the nights were getting colder) and set the place on fire.

Tanaquil, the farmer, and his men, these in slippers and cursing, had managed to put the fire out, despite the peeve, who leapt excitedly round their ankles and almost tripped them up. Tanaquil paid for the damage. She went off under the usual cloud of disapproval, her 'blasted nuisance dog' as the farmer had titled the peeve, trotting blamelessly by the camel's side.

After this, the peeve would not let brush or comb near it. In any case, it was possible, she thought, that Worabex in flea-shape had now removed himself to the woolly camel.

Whatever else, all this kept her mind on other things than loss. And besides, she thought she might be relieved, nostalgic, even happy, to reach *home*. Home being the fortress where she had grown up.

Tanaquil even began to look forward, perhaps, to meeting her mother again.

Jaive was beautiful and essentially a good person, but she was careless, reckless, mad, a sorceress, and had always seemed uninterested in Tanaquil—until the very last moment. The moment when Tanaquil and Jaive both discovered Tanaquil was too, in her way, a talented witch.

Once in the desert, picking their route from their map with caution, Tanaquil would take out the emerald necklace she had kept for Jaive from Lizra's unwanted presents, and look at it by the light of the moon. Could a mother refound compensate for the true love of your life that you had had to give up? No, but she might help. They had that in common now, after all. Tanaquil's father had abandoned Jaive. Though Honj and Tanaquil had agreed they must part for Lizra's sake, heartbreak, whatever the cause, could be sympathetic ground.

Maybe she and Jaive could talk about it, and that *would* help both of them.

So long, of course, as the mighty Worabex, that commanding, overpowering know-all, did not interfere too much.

The night before the day before they should arrive at the fortress, the peeve spruced itself before the fire.

Overhead the sky was blue as indigo, speckled with stars, and set with a huge moon. The night was icy, and the light snow rimmed the dunes. Tanaquil sat breathing in the somehow forgotten scents.

"All gone," announced the peeve.

"Oh yes . . . sorry, what?"

"All gone," repeated the peeve. It rose, and stood like a burnished fur barrel, its feet planted firmly, ears up, tail up, eyes beaming firelight.

"What's all gone? Your supper? Do you want something else?"

"Not," said the peeve. "No flea."

Tanaquil observed it. A shiver of apprehension went over her. "You mean, are you saying you've caught *all* your fleas?"

"All."

"Are you . . . sure?"

"Find and snap. Yip," said the peeve. "Want look?" it added winningly.

"That's all right. But surely—"

The peeve frowned, which somehow it had recently learned to do. By watching Tanaquil frowning at everything? *"None,"* it said.

She thought. Could the peeve have groomed out and eaten *Worabex*?

That must be impossible, though serve him right if it had tried. But he was a great magician, this had to be admitted. Probably he was cunningly hiding somewhere in the peeve or camel's coats, keeping utterly still, vile with smugness, and sophisticated adult amusement.

In the morning, soon after sunrise and breakfast, they went on towards the fortress. The peeve, sitting bolt upright on the camel's neck, was the first to make the building out. The peeve uttered loud squeaks and grunts, wordless for once. Tanaquil looked harder, and saw a mass of rock that might only be a mesa. It was the same baked-cake shade as the sand. But then roofs glimmered greenishly, and you saw chimneys, and weathervanes that gleamed and flashed.

Tanaquil was home. Was she?

As if she must anyway act out enthusiasm, Tanaquil put the camel into a fast lope. By now, she supposed, as they swung in from the sands, someone would have seen her. Hopefully Jaive's drunken soldiers would not take aim and fire their crossbows or cannon. Most outsiders, to them, might be fearful enemies. Perhaps they were still asleep.

No sound came from the fort. Not a wisp of smoke from any still-simmering chimney.

It looked so strange. So new. As if Tanaquil had never seen it before. But how could that be? How long had she been away? Not even two years.

Just then a pink firework, perfectly visible on the day sky, shot up into the air and broke into a rain of spangles.

"Oh, *Mother*!" Tanaquil exclaimed, annoyed. This at least was only too familiar. And then—and then Tanaquil thought, *Is that because she knows it's me? Is that a welcome?*

But when she had come to the vast and imposing main doors, which never in all her time there had she ever used before, they swung wide to reveal, not Jaive at all.

"Good morning, Tanaquil," expansively and so kindly said Worabex the magician.

"How fascinating. You got here ahead of me."

"By at least a week."

Obviously, if he had wanted to impress Jaive, and he had previously made it rather clear he might want to, he would not arrive as a *flea*.

Wrapped up in her own life, Tanaquil had not properly worked this out.

Beyond the big doors, that would have been stiff and creaky but for magic, a large, ornamentally arched court-yard offered a flight of steps. These ended at the fortress's main inner door. Tanaquil was not surprised to see one of the stone lions on the steps twitching its tail rapidly.

"How's my mother?"

"Jaive is very well. We've been expecting you, naturally. She's giving a feast tonight in your honor."

"Oh, lovely."

"I see your face has fallen. Believe me, Tanaquil, this feast will be worthy of anything seen on your travels. After the servants left, a more effective service was put—"

"Excuse me. The servants left?"

"Really, the change will be wonderful for them."

"*When* did they leave?" asked Tanaquil.

"About four days ago."

"About three days after your arrival."

Worabex smiled pleasantly. He was as she had seen him last on her journey, middle-aged but tall and strong, quite athletic in build, with an absolute mane of black, gray-frosted hair, and a bold handsome face. If this was his real appearance, or only one designed to entrance her mother, it had been apparently effective.

Tanaquil glared at him.

"What did you do to the servants? Some of them had been here before I was born. Prune and Yeefa . . . the cook . . . my poor old nurse—"

"The old nurse is still in residence. She's very glamorous now. You'll be interested."

"Pillow had a *child*. Have you just thrown them all out, or did you and my mother do something so truly awful they ran away?"

"There was a small caravan of traders. They went with those. All were well rewarded. A small fortune, from your mother's coffers. You're really taking this much too seriously. People sometimes want a change in their lives. After all, dear girl, a sorceress of your mother's capability hardly needs *human* assistants."

"I think," said Tanaquil, "she kept them here for company. Human *warmth*. I mean, when she noticed them."

"Yes," said Worabex, "you've always been your mother's sternest critic, haven't you?"

Tanaquil literally bit her tongue to stop her flow of verbal anger. It was no use talking to him. And now they had reached the top of the lion flight, and the stone lions were all flicking their tails and yawning, and licking their paws, in a showy way. She was out of breath. The calm camel stood below, drinking steadily from a trough of cool water. Worabex had supplied the water with a click of his fingers.

The peeve had vanished at the doors outside, snuffling down and off along the dunes. At least, it was glad to be here, but then all places were alike to it, full of potential, questions, and absurd delights.

Tanaquil paused in the door's blue shadow. She listened. It was so *quiet*.

"I suppose," she said, "you sent the soldiers packing too."

Worabex raised one eyebrow. He would.

"Most of them have left. One or two . . . well, they're lazy drunkards, rather silly, aren't they? No one would want them. So these remained."

Tanaquil, furious, could not stop herself. "You're the sternest critic of the soldiers, then."

"I don't criticize them, I simply see what they are. The world needs fools as well as genius."

"*Why?*"

"For balance."

Tanaquil had a mental picture, Prune, Yeefa, Pillow, Pillow's noisy child, Bird, the kindly cook . . . the funny, tipsy soldiers who were always so tactful, so nice to Tanaquil . . . the old men who had been retainers since the days probably of Jaive's own mother. All of them tramping out into the barren sand with their bundles, and the crossbows done up in brown paper. Her eyes filled with tears, but whether of pain or rage she was not sure. She had sometimes lost patience with these people.

Worabex had gone on into the wide passage beyond the door, and stood waiting.

Tanaquil recalled this part of the fortress only vaguely. Perhaps it had even been altered.

Just then, drifting over the courtyard, came a gauzy sparkly thing, unmistakably some sort of demon. It alighted on the camel, and gently but firmly rode it through an arch, presumably to be stabled. The camel, a cynic, made no trouble.

"So the new servants are all demons?" said Tanaquil sweetly.

"What else," said Worabex, "in the house of a sorceress, would you expect?"

Nothing, thought Tanaquil. *Absolutely nothing else.*

II

Tanaquil was not given her old room, the room she had known for sixteen years.

Instead, another dainty, gauzy, half-transparent thing with the head of a deer, led her up to a guest chamber. Here everything worked, even the silver taps shaped like bell-flowers in the bathroom. Hot water splashed into a marble tub and Tanaquil presently lay soaking, having shouted the deer-thing rudely from the room.

No doubt she had seen the guest suite before. She must have done. But she did not remember its ice-cream-green walls with little jewel-like paintings of palaces and gardens. The large bed with its sunrise-colored canopy looked itself new as a morning. When you pressed a golden lever, a flight of adorable blue birds flew over the ceiling. Rather like something similar in the royal bedroom of Lizra, when Lizra was only a princess by the sea.

After the bath, Tanaquil found a table laid with tea and wine and cake. None of this turned into anything else, as food so often had done in former times, although one of the marble columns of the fireplace had changed into an orange tree with ripening fruit. Perhaps that was deliberate, anyway.

So far, Tanaquil had not seen Jaive. She had thought Worabex was taking her to Jaive. But when the deer-thing appeared and beckoned her, bowing, Worabex explained that she would see Jaive this evening, just before the feast.

Tanaquil said, "I have a right to see my mother now."

"Do you? She has, of course, a right also. And Jaive suggested she would meet you before dinner."

Tanaquil felt herself flush as red as her hair.

As she did so, she recalled only too vividly running away with the black unicorn, staying away with the gold unicorn. Although her adventures had not been entirely of her own choosing, she had left Jaive and not gone back at the time she had said she would. Jaive could be exasperating, but she was not stupid. Jaive must know Tanaquil had put other matters first, other people.

She thought of the—rather pompous?—letter she had written to Jaive nearly two years ago: "We'll have things to talk about. You'll have to trust me, please."

The last time they had spoken face to face, Jaive had been standing on the ocean, or her illusion had.

"Tanaquil, you're a sorceress."

"Of course I'm not."

But Jaive had proved it to her.

And Jaive had been beautiful and warm . . . and proud of her.

But after that came so much. They had lost each other again. *I lose them all, don't I? Mother, sister, love.*

Tanaquil ate some cake and drank the tea. She went to the window and opened the immaculate glass. Below was the old garden court she remembered, with vines and palm tree, and three fawn escaped goats grazing peacefully on a rose bush. Not everything had altered, then.

Tonight, when she met her mother, Tanaquil must make an effort. She wondered where the peeve was, but going to open her travelling bag in the dressing alcove, she found a dress on a stand, obviously intended for the dinner.

Tanaquil forgot the peeve. She forgot Jaive on the ocean.

"Oh, *Mother.* For goodness *sake.*"

As she climbed the stairs that evening to her mother's sorcerium, Tanaquil, busy managing the dress, was conscious of the carvings on the wooden banisters, which, oddly, were keeping completely still. Conscious too, on the landings, of the openings to the roof walks and battlements, empty of soldiers.

When she reached the big black door, Tanaquil stopped and waited, looking at the head of green jade. But instead of its usual superfluous questions, the head said to her, "Welcome, Tanaquil." And the door, without its recollected creak, swung wide.

The chamber beyond smelled of smoke, fire, spices, furry animals, electricity, and wild invention. But it looked quite tidy. Books were stacked upon the chests with markers dripping from them. Veils hung over magical mirrors. Much clutter had been put from sight, and only two purple kittens were playing with a ball under Jaive's impressive worktable. On which only one glass bubble let off little puffs of soft steam.

Jaive stood behind the table.

She was alone. Tanaquil had been thinking Worabex might be there with her. In a way, he was.

Tanaquil's mother looked radiant. She wore a gown of plain rich silk the shade of the kittens, and a delicate necklace formed like a golden snake holding its own tail in its mouth. The scarlet hair was smooth as the stillest pool.

"Here you are," said Jaive. "How are you?"

"Here," said Tanaquil.

Jaive gave a little laugh. Tanaquil realized with uncomfortable unsurprised surprise that her mother seemed to be nervous.

"I meant . . ."

"I know. I'm sorry. It's simply that . . . *he*—" Tanaquil broke off. Without even hearing the name *Worabex*, Jaive was prettily blushing, like a girl of sixteen. She was a great deal older than that.

Well, why shouldn't she like him?

Tanaquil frowned. She thought of the peeve learning to frown from constantly watching her frown.

"I'd hoped to see you first. That's all."

"But," said Jaive, "you must have been tired."

"Not really."

Perhaps this was not quite true. Tanaquil had spent some of the day asleep on the green and gold guest bed.

"Anyway. Now we meet. After so long."

"Yes. I'm sorry."

"He . . . told me about it."

"Oh. Did he?"

"You've had extraordinary experiences, Tanaquil. Just as a sorceress should."

"So I'm finally measuring up," Tanaquil snapped. She shook herself. "This is silly. Shouldn't I kiss you? I've brought you a present."

Jaive looked at her. "That's very kind."

Oh God, now she's gone all remote and polite.

Tanaquil moved forward, with difficulty, and put down the emerald necklace, carefully wrapped in emerald paper tied with a velvet bow.

"What lovely wrapping! Shall I open it?"

"Or just put it in some cupboard." Tanaquil grimaced. "I'm *sorry*. This is awful, isn't it? If you'd rather open it when I'm not here . . . Mother, why this *dreadful dress*?"

Jaive's mouth fell ajar.

"I thought purple would be festive."

"Not *your* dress. You look sensational. You always do. But *this* for *me*—"

Tanaquil balanced there, held hard and breathless by the boned waist of the garment. It was red copper in color, flounced and embroidered, with a hem two inches thick in gold. From the sleeves exploded out undersleeves that felt as heavy as iron from pearls and gold and beads.

"You look beautiful in it," said Jaive, very cold now. "I chose the colors for your hair."

"Mother, I'm *not* beautiful."

"You are," said Jaive frozenly. "Of course you are."

Below, as in days long gone, the dinner gong sounded, raucous and inappropriate.

Jaive shook back her hair. Suspended upside down from

each ear was a small black bat with silver-tipped wings,
fluttering quietly. How typical.

"We must go down," said Jaive, "to the feast."

Tanaquil felt angry and apologetic. She felt ashamed of
herself. She had wanted to say a thousand things. Instead—

"Just stand with me on this carpet," Jaive was saying, gra-
ciously.

Numbly Tanaquil moved on to it, trying not to fall over
flounces and goldwork.

"Down, slave," commanded Jaive.

The carpet plunged.

Tanaquil had a horrible sickening vision of stone dis-
solving and flying off, walls, stairs, doors rushing past. Her
mother stood in the midst, a pillar of purple and fire.

They landed in the dining room with a flurry of sparks
and vapors, to the loud applause of the assembled guests.

Tanaquil, swallowing her stomach, had now very little
left to say, and none of it particularly friendly. In all the
days of her youth, Jaive had *never* employed such a device.

Jaive's hall had always been drafty. Now it was not, it was
cosily but refreshingly warm. In three fireplaces burned
green and red fires. The silk curtains were without a tear
or darn. The enormous round window of red and emerald glass—broken by the exit of the black unicorn—had
been tidily restored.

Worabex sat at the table's centre, at Jaive's right hand.
Both had ebony chairs.

Everyone else had chairs heavily plated with silver.

Worabex had come towards Tanaquil and Jaive after

the carpet landed, and offered to each an arm. They went sailing to the table covered with exquisite cloth, crystal, gold, gemmed cups, and a dozen other royal-looking objects.

Tanaquil had wanted to refuse the arm of Worabex, but thought it better not to. The occasion was heavy with a sense of Proper Behavior, shades of the court of Prince Zorander, worse—of Lizra's military dinners, which only Honj had lightened. Honj.

Tanaquil now found herself seated by Worabex. On Jaive's other side, as they sat down, she saw the captain of the soldiers, and his second-in-command. They wore their gilded mothball-scented mail and sashes, pinned with all their battle honors that might even be real. They were stiff as posts, with angry pale faces. Not even drunk. But the captain suddenly got up, and strode to Tanaquil's chair.

"A great happiness to see you here, lady," said the captain.

Tanaquil pushed back her own chair and rose. She held out her hand and he clasped it in both of his. His eyes looked bleak and wounded. What had the magician done to him? Taken away the little pride he had left?

And then the captain glanced sidelong at Jaive, nestled next to Worabex, flushed and lovely, offering him wine from a crystal flagon.

The captain said, "You'll find us changed, ma'am."

"Yes. I have."

The captain's second had also come up. He clanked his heels together and bowed.

"Madam is very taken up with new things," he said, in a hoarse, resentful low tone.

A look of understanding passed between Tanaquil and the soldiers. Tanaquil said, quite clearly, "It's always good when *old* friends aren't forgotten in the pleasure of making *new* ones."

The captain's eyes sparkled for a moment.

"There you have it, lady."

Worabex and Jaive seemed not to have noticed.

The two bats had flown down from Jaive's ears, and she was letting them lick drops of wine from her fingers, while Worabex admiringly gazed at her.

Then there was a fanfare. A pair of demons of the gauzy type, with elephant's heads, blew it by means of their trunks. Other charming demons came in through the doors, and the feast began.

It was, you had to admit, impressive.

All the demons were of the gently cute-looking sort, with the heads of animals—deer, cats, elephants, horses. They did everything efficiently, somehow *smilingly,* and from them wafted perfumes. You wanted to hit them.

To add to the rarity of the dinner, all the colossal tureens and salvers were borne each upon a single giant feather. Gulls' for the fish, flamingoes' for the ices, the towering roasts each on an eagle's plume, and the myriad stunning desserts that completed the extravagant nine courses, upon iridescent peacocks' feathers. Nor did the demons in any way support these feathers, simply steered them balletically along through the air to the table, where they floated down, then withdrew, untouched, from the steaming, gleaming dishes.

With every course came different colored wines and juices. If the performance itself had not made her sick, thought Tanaquil, the feast would have done. But she ate very little, and now and then shot the captain—drunk at last—worried glances as he stuffed huge helpings of everything down his throat.

There was another little problem, too. The second-in-command had turned out allergic to the feathers. The poor fellow spent most of the meal trying to scratch himself, unseen, and sneezing into a big mauve handkerchief.

But Jaive and Worabex took no notice.

Nor was there any of the former ritual of saluting the dishes. Jaive was too busy discussing everything with her beloved, and he with her. The feast, it seemed, had been constructed sorcerously, hence its sumptuous abundance. Yet it was utterly convincing, the fish clean and fresh, the meat flavorsome and rich, the apple and chocolate puddings delicious to the point of insanity.

"A-*chaugh!*" bellowed the second-in-command for the forty-fifth time, and a salt cellar set with rubies rolled onto the floor.

Farther down the table the other three guests took very little notice either of anyone else. They were old people, all three, and Tanaquil had seen before that sometimes the very old, as with the very young, had little real interest in any but their own peers.

The two ladies were elegant, slender and upright, and dressed in glamorous gowns. The old man wore dreadful, filthy clothes that gladdened Tanaquil's heart. She recognized him as the gravy steward of Jaive's former dinners, about the time she recognized that the ladies were her old nurse, and the fish stewardess. All three had long grey hair, and the women had wound theirs with pearls and diamonds. There was no denying they looked well and attractive, in a way she did not recall, a bloom on their lined cheeks, their eyes bright. They were strong too, cracking walnuts with their teeth, (surely the nurse had lost her teeth?) and once having a playful, and dangerous, little fight with the meat knives.

"A-*chuff*!"

"My nurse looks very fit," said Tanaquil to Worabex.

"Your nurse? Oh, yes."

"You cast some spell for her? I thought you believed it was wrong to interfere with things like aging or finance or the environment. Yet there she is with all her teeth."

"Perhaps I wouldn't want to make her young," said Worabex, turning regretfully from Jaive, who was feeding her bats apple pudding. "There's no disgrace in growing old. But why shouldn't one enjoy one's old age? I removed the stiffness in their joints, improved their circulation and digestion, hearing, eyesight, and so on. And yes, some teeth grew back."

"Did they ask you to do that?"

"Obviously they did."

"They never thought to ask Jaive."

Worabex said, softly, "There are some spells that I have been able to share with your mother."

"You mean she couldn't have done it, and you can."

"Jaive is also able to perform magics that I've never learned."

"A-*choof*!"

"Perhaps you could take away that poor man's allergy."

"Perhaps the poor man doesn't want me to."

Tanaquil swore. When she did so, Worabex laughed.

The gravy steward of eighty-eight was removing the cork from a bottle with his teeth.

Worabex turned back to Jaive.

A final dish had appeared, simply materialized on the table. It was the savory which concluded the meal.

Tanaquil sat bolt upright, held by the boned dress. She would not look at her mother and her mother's lover. She thought, *I'm like some disapproving parent.*

After the savory, the guests got up and walked about, although how some of them could move after all the food was a mystery.

Music played in the air, and Jaive and Worabex began to dance, holding each other's hands. Then the steward invited the stewardess, and they danced too, limber as thirty-year-olds.

The captain rose and came staggering to Tanaquil. "May I have the *hic* the honor?"

Although she had learned dancing on her travels, Tanaquil could see he was in no state to dance.

"I'm too tired, Captain. But please sit here with me."

He sank into the chair. It had been Worabex's.

"A-ach-*plaush*!"

"Do you think he needs some fresh air?"

"He's all right. Good man. Stuck with me. Stayed. Nothing for us here. Oughta go."

"Then you should," said Tanaquil.

"Well, y'see," said the captain. He lowered his eyes and one startling drunk tear rolled down his cheek. "All these years here, guarding her. I've always . . . she used to rely on *me.*"

He loves her, thought Tanaquil in horrified realization.

All the time, he loved her. And now—what a mess.

As Jaive and Worabex returned to the table, the second-in-command jumped up and managed to sneeze with astounding violence all over the magician.

The captain winked sadly at Tanaquil. "Saved himself for that."

Abruptly she remembered how Honj had deliberately caught the feasting peeve's sneeze in an appalled noble's hat. Honj—

The peeve.

Where was it? She had forgotten it. She had not seen it since this morning.

III

When she was with Honj, his soldiers, the Locusts, had reminded her of the soldiers of Jaive's fortress. Now the captain and his second reminded her, of course, of Honj's men. So she *liked* being with them. The first thing she *had* liked here.

Wandering about in the frosty night sands below Jaive's fortress, the second carrying a torch, they were searching for the peeve.

As they completed their circuit and started round a second time, she saw again the red and green window of the hall, glowing only five feet above the dunes. It was impossible to see in through the panes, though faint music still sounded.

The captain looked miserable, and Tanaquil was afraid, after all the food and drink, he would be ill. As if sensing her thought, the second announced, "One good thing about that stinker's magic meals—no hangover."

The second had stopped sneezing promptly following his last magnificent effort. Tanaquil had almost laughed, watching him brushing Worabex down with the wet mauve hanky, saying, "Oh pardon me, sir, what a ghastly thing," etc.

They had all laughed when they got outside, before gloom returned.

"Any chance it could have run off?" added the second. "I mean, it's a peeve."

"No, not really. My familiar, you see," said Tanaquil. Here, of all places, they would understand that.

"Oh, right. Well, no sign yet."

Tanaquil was worried. She told herself that the peeve, as she was, had become invulnerable. Nothing surely could hurt it. But supposing it were trapped somewhere?

She called, "Peeeeve!" This sounded daft. Then they all did it. Dafter.

"I think probably," she said, "it's just gone off exploring old haunts. It can usually find me. Sometimes it was missing for a while. I'll leave my window open. . . . Thank you anyway. You've been kind."

They always had been kind in her childhood. Finding her things to mend when she was going mad with boredom. Tonight, the captain had mentioned the cannon she had mended, twice.

They went round to a door and idled there. Tanaquil looked towards the rock hills, half a mile off. The moon was up, half full, and touched them with gilt. It was *there* she had found—the peeve had found—the bones of the black unicorn, from the Perfect World. And so begun all this.

Could the peeve be there?

But she could not ask these weary, fed-up men to go that

way, and if she said she would go they would feel they must. She would have to trust the peeve. After all, there had been times, as she said, it had gone off in other lands, in unknown cities, in strange countryside. Though perhaps it had never been missing for as long as this.

"You go in," said the captain to his second. "I'd just like a word with Lady Tanaquil, if she won't mind."

The second clicked his heels again, and went off.

"What is it, captain?"

"Well, I don't know how to ask you, frankly."

Tanaquil braced herself. She knew he was going to speak about her mother. But at last he looked her directly in the eyes. He said, flatly, "I understand your sorcery is in mending, madam. Well, you always could mend things beautifully." He paused, swallowed. He said, "Can you mend a broken heart?"

"Oh, captain." Was it a witty joke? No, for he looked deadly serious. "I don't think it's the same thing," she said.

"The old stinker," he too meant Worabex, "said you mended some chap's broken arm."

Honj . . . "That was a bone, though. I don't—"

"I know the heart doesn't actually break, madam. Just feels as if it has. In bits. I don't know where I am. I never asked anything from her, you see. I made do with just looking out for her. Now I'm as much use as the cannon. The fortress is *sorcerously* guarded. If a friend approaches, up goes a pink firework. And a red one for an enemy. Then the demons get ready. Or so he says."

"My mother," said Tanaquil, "valued you very highly."

"Did she? Yes, perhaps. Not any more."

As he was speaking, Tanaquil seemed to see right into

his chest, and there the heart was, not as it would be in fact, but an exact symbolic heart shape, and made of pure gold. It had cracked in two.

She thought, maybe sympathetic magic might help after all. And the old challenge—why *not*? She said to him, "I'll try."

She put her hand flat on the captain's chest, where in her imagination she could see the broken golden heart.

She visualized the heart coming together, sealing tight. In a moment it was done. Now the heart had only one honorable scar.

Some pain it seemed you had to suffer. But this pain would only wear him out. It would be no use. She said in her mind to the healed heart, *Be free. Be whole. Be ready for another.*

Then she stepped back.

The captain blinked in the moonlight.

"The God," he said. Then he smiled. He looked younger. "Like a ton weight lifting off me. You *are* good, aren't you? What a girl, er, madam. Yes. Jaive's a fine woman. Good luck to her. But, plenty more fish in the sea."

He turned in at the door, and held it wide for her.

As they walked through the corridor, he whistled under his breath. At the foot of the stairs, he said, "I can't thank you enough. You've really helped me."

"I'm glad. I hope so. Don't . . . be disappointed if . . ."

"I'll sleep on it. If I feel like this tomorrow, I'll be off. And my second will go with me. I mean, if we've gone, you'll know I'm all right."

Yet one more pang of loss went through Tanaquil. This her reward for helping, to lose her only friend.

He mistook her expression.

"I really think you've done it." He shook her hand now. Then leaned and kissed her cheek. "The best of fortune to you, lady. You deserve great happiness."

As she climbed the stairs, she thought, *If I healed his broken heart, why not mine?* But she knew then she wanted the pain. It was all she had left of Honj.

About an hour before sunrise, the peeve came in through her opened window. She woke as it plopped down hard on her stomach.

"Where have you *been?*"

"Mpp," said the peeve. It looked extremely sheepish, actually embarrassed. What had it done? But she fell asleep again, with its sandy-smelling snoring fur under her chin. And in the morning, going up to the battlements, Tanaquil found no one. While from the turret where the captain had lived, everything was gone. He had left her a note, or left everyone a note. It was scratched into the wall. It read:

Plenty more fish in the sea for me.

IV

So she kept the pain.

It was all she had of him.

And she thought of him every morning, almost, for five or ten, sometimes for twenty or thirty minutes. And then she tried to put him out of her mind for the rest of the day.

How dull yet irritating the days were, too. Like the time here, before she had run away. Jaive shut up in the sorcerium, or dawdling through the fortress with Worabex. Shouts of laughter. Bangs of random magic. Apples changing into lemons, lemons changing to mice, an ostrich running through the corridors *bleating*. A rainbow that dropped down colors that stained everything for a whole afternoon. Like before, worse than before.

While the peeve—the peeve was definitely up to something.

Most nights it was absent, from sunset until sunrise, or longer. During the day it went missing too. It gave off, rather than its usual air of busyness, a sly, furtive, secrecy. She had not said to it, "Where do you go? What do you do?" She thought it was out exploring. Yet, this odd human guiltiness hung round it. It was *shifty*.

And, on the other hand, it was always appearing and trying to cheer her up, distract her, feed her. Somehow it constantly rustled up or stole bits of bread, cheese, squashy fruits. Probably these were leftovers from the dinners or breakfasts the magician and sorceress shared. Tanaquil, to please the peeve, tended to eat what it brought in preference to the elaborate dishes left by the demons outside the guest room door. (She had . . . persuaded the demons not to come in at all, ever.)

In the first couple of days after the captain and his second had gone away, Tanaquil had roamed about the fortress. She had seen the empty basement kitchen, already thick with blown-in sand and spiderwebs. Neither Jaive nor Worabex nor the demons needed to employ anything as ordinary as a kitchen. Imagined pictures of the cook, the kitchen boys, Pillow's child with her mended doll, hovered in the air.

Other parts of the fortress seemed changed, as Tanaquil had first suspected. Some chambers, before neglected, had blossomed with rich furnishings and mechanical toys. Some rooms seemed to have disappeared or been relocated. The garden courtyard, viewed even from the guest window, had some new trees, with singing flowers or silver fruits growing on them. The goats, always now in some mode of escape, occasionally got into the fortress. But they allowed the demons to milk them. This was done for the goats' own comfort, not because their milk was needed. The pails of white liquid stood in corners, turning to cheese, until the demons came back and vanished them with a wave. Once the peeve, suddenly appearing, got to one first and drank half the bucket, before the demon shooed it off. It was useless for the peeve to try to bite the demon. All of them were physically insubstantial. In case the demon might retaliate, however, Tanaquil dragged the peeve away.

"You look very smart," said Tanaquil to the peeve, not really thinking. "Very combed."

"Yes. Much groom." It gave her a look, went "Sprr," and bounded abruptly off.

Only later did it occur to her the peeve had seemed to think it had just made some sort of mistake. As if to be *groomed* was an error.

At dinner it reappeared, as it normally did, never, incredibly, seeming interested at all in the tray of delicacies at the door, bringing Tanaquil today one very beautiful green fig.

"Thank you. That *is* nice. Sweet." She ate it, and the peeve sat on the floor, now and then turning round, twiddling its tail. "If you want to go out again, please go ahead."

"Out? Just in."

"Yes. But you don't seem settled."

The peeve jumped up on the bed, turned a somersault, ran up a curtain, fell down another curtain, and gained the window embrasure.

"Big moon," said the peeve.

"Yes, it's full tonight."

"Just must—" said the peeve, and scrambled over the edge, rummaging off across the roofs again.

She thought, *Did it ever know a full moon was coming before?* It had always seemed keen on the moon, but surprised by the moon. Maybe it had learned the moon's phases.

In a small stable court the camel was well cared for, fed and watered, even exercised by demons. Tanaquil did not like this, but she realized she had neglected the camel. It really was going to be no use lying on her bed or walking up and down corridors, thinking of Honj all day. It had been supposed to be five minutes for Honj.

As for Jaive, since the feast, Tanaquil had *met* her. That had to be the term. Met. No more arranged gatherings. She would simply come on Jaive and Worabex, always together, in some room or passage, as when chasing the bleating ostrich, for example, with screams of adolescent mirth. They made her feel very old.

She noticed that they now wore simple, spell-stained garments. Jaive's hair was again a mess, and once—just once—Tanaquil was sure she saw a mousp tangled up in the mane of Worabex.

Another time, she discovered them having a sumptuous picnic on a staircase, with all the carvings flying round them. The wooden vultures were catching bits of meat, that Worabex threw for them, on the wing.

"Oh, Tanaquil. Do come and have some—"

"Er, no, thanks. I'm just going . . . to my room for . . . something."

But they did not look sad when she left them there. She was quite superfluous.

On one occasion, too, she came upon her glamorous old nurse. *She* was dressed up in cloth-of-gold, with high-heeled slippers, and two pet rats with pearl necklets. The peeve, luckily, was elsewhere.

"How have you been?"

"Lovely, dear. And who are you?"

Fearing that the old woman's memory had failed her after all, Tanaquil explained who she was.

"Oh *that* Tanaquil," said the nurse, cuttingly. "You've aged, dear."

She then strode vigorously off on her three-inch heels, the rats skidding after her. Tanaquil distinctly heard one rat say, *"Who that?"* The other replied, *"I dunno. Who care?"*

Which meant that at last the rats too had caught the knack of speech, and also that no one, absolutely none of them, cared about her.

She had come back to be at least dutiful, perhaps, daughterly. But she was redundant. Had ten or twelve days passed, or more? Surely, it was already time to go.

But where? To whom? To what?

Tanaquil was dreaming. She knew she was. The desert stretched away from her mother's fortress, covered in layers of deep crimson, peach pink and purple flowers. And over this a unicorn ran towards her.

She felt great happiness seeing it. It had not forgotten her. Conceivably, it needed her for something.

Then, as the sun rose higher in her dream, Tanaquil saw it was not either of the unicorns she had known before. Not the black unicorn with its moon-sea-fire mane, nor even the gold steam-driven unicorn of Lizra's war.

This unicorn was russet red.

The mane, the tail, the fringes of the fetlocks, were of a strange greenish bronze.

But its horn was red copper, the very color of some dress Tanaquil had worn, sometime, recently.

Nevertheless, a unicorn it was. It spun over the flowery sands, coming straight at her. And all at once she saw the metallic horn was levelled at her heart.

Something hit exactly there. She shouted and sat up, and the dream fell down in fragments like a broken mirror.

It was just sunrise. The peeve, outlined with soft gold, was rolling down the bed, having landed on her quite hard a moment before.

"Don't *do* that."

"Sorry."

"It's all right. Just don't. Though I'm glad you woke me."

The peeve righted itself and washed rapidly. Shook itself. It lifted its front paw. Its topaz eyes were huge.

"Found something."

"What?" Tanaquil felt slow. Her mind was already racing.

"Want show."

In this way it had come to her, bringing the moonlight bone of the first unicorn.

She said, before she could think, "From the rock hills, the arch like the unicorn gate, do you mean from there?"

The peeve's eyes bulged.

"Whup."

"Is that a yes?"

"Come see," said the peeve. Then it blinked and looked down. "No. Me tell first."

Enthralled, tingling with excitement and hope, she leaned forward.

"Tell me, then."

"Was playing. Then she. We play. Play good. Then hunt. Then I go rock, and play there, with she."

"Wait," said Tanaquil, "*she*? Who?" She sounded like the nurse's rat.

The peeve began to search carefully, virtuously, for a flea. It turned round, tumbled over, raised a back leg, snorted.

"Who is *she*?" impatiently said Tanaquil. She was only puzzled. And yet, within her, the sudden hope-flame, dying . . .

"Name Adma. Have name. Not speak. From rocks. Nice. Sweet."

"*Adma?*"

"Nice."

Tanaquil, bemused, sat back, but she was cold inside, and heavy. It was as if part of her had turned to stone.

The peeve raised its head. It stared at Tanaquil, fierce, defiant. *Human.*

"Mine," said the peeve. "My *girl.*"

After Tanaquil had washed and dressed and put on her boots, and drunk some of the tea left by the door, and after the peeve had upset a bowl of raisin and nut porridge and washed and dressed in *that*, they went to meet the peeve's 'girl.'

Tanaquil's heart—and she could visualize it—was like lead. But she tried to seem bright and pleased.

The peeve, no fool, now said little.

There was a way over the roofs, and Tanaquil and the

peeve climbed out, and around. After a while Tanaquil grasped they had come up, over gulleys and slopes and flat bits, to the eave of the library. The peeve led her through the dry canal between the roofs where red flowers grew, past the old cistern.

"Is it your original nest?" Tanaquil asked politely.

"Yes, good nest."

They had to jump the tiny space with the large drop below. There was no one in the kitchen yard down there, no one hanging out washing. And no soldiers scanned them, nervous or drunk, from the battlements.

The ancient ravens' nest was all gone. They went by the place, then the peeve said, "Go ahead me. Tell her you coming."

"Oh yes, of course."

He—foolish to continue saying *it*—he rattled away down the channel.

After a minute she heard him squeak, and then his most soprano call. He used her name. *"Tanaquil!"* Had the peeve called her by name ever before?

And she was to go in alone. He was waiting there with his friend. His mate.

Under the dark overhang, she came to the peeve nest. It was expectedly full of things, cushions, brushes, meat bones, jewelry stolen—presumably—from Jaive or the old women. It had the familiar smell of musky fur and warmth.

Bolt upright sat the peeve. And, just behind him, another peeve. Who must be Adma.

She was smaller, her pelt a little more blonde. One of the wild peeves that lived normally by the rock hills, she did not, he said, speak. Both her paws were down, but her ears were up and her tail was very, very bushy. Either she was anxious or angry. Her eyes were the roundest, most brilliant jewels in the nest.

Tanaquil looked at the female peeve.

Did she understand human speech? Had the peeve taught her? Would she want to be talked to as Tanaquil talked to the peeve, or in a more . . . *animal* way? Definitely *not* oochy-coochy-coo.

"Hallo," said Tanaquil. She added lamely, "Your nest is very nice."

Adma's tail got bigger, then smoothed off. Her eyes seemed to soften. She made a soft, cautious chirrup.

The peeve said, proudly, "She says you smell all right."

"Oh, er, thank you."

Tanaquil, gazing about uneasily, noticed bits of a familiar rug ripped up and wedged in among the cushion stuffing and garnets. She decided not to mention this.

But now what?

"May I . . . stroke you?" asked Tanaquil of the female peeve. "Adma?" This could be quite the wrong approach.

But the peeve chattered to Adma.

Adma spoke back in peeve talk.

"Says proper sniff first."

"You mean do *I*, or does *she*—"

The peeve said, "Give hand."

So Tanaquil kneeled and held out her hand. Now she would be bitten. Adma snuffed at her with a firm wet nose, licked her, considered, and then gave a squeak.

"Stroke, stroke," enthused the peeve, generously.

Tanaquil stroked Adma, who was marvellously silky. When Adma had had enough, she turned her back, and puttered off deeper into the nest.

"Go feed Adma now," said the peeve. He indicated the tufts of porridge stuck on his coat. "Glad met."

"Yes, it was. . . . Thanks. She's, er, pretty."

But the peeve was waddling off over the picked bones, and the shreds of Jaive's magic carpet. Dimly, down the channel, Tanaquil saw and heard them, the two peeves, mutually grooming.

The best visitor never outstays her welcome.

Before she went back to the guest suite, Tanaquil went over and looked in at her own old bedroom. The shutters were off, and the chamber quite vacant, nothing in it at all. Not even the sorcerous talking portrait of her mother. She could just see the lion's head in the bathing alcove. It had always been more likely to dispense chicken soup or ribbons rather than water, but now it had a choked and dried-up look.

She sat on the sill.

Why had she never thought the peeve might find its— his—own companion? He had every right to do so. And obviously now, he did not need Tanaquil at all. Tanaquil was only an interruption.

She turned and looked away towards the rocks. To shut up this book that was her finished early life, Tanaquil might need to walk out there. Scrutinize the place where the bones of the first unicorn had lain. One last time.

But when she got back to the guest chamber, and was climbing in the window, she was met by a jelly pink, doe-

faced demon that had squeezed in through the closed
door.

"The sorceress wishes you to come and lunch with her."

"Very well," said Tanaquil. It would be a chance to say
good-bye, for once, in a civilized way.

V

This room Tanaquil did not recall, but maybe it had been there like others, simply made different. At the center of a table piled with delicacies, was an icy frothing mountain stream in miniature, pouring out of nothing and away into nothing, and in the midst of it stood a large cooling bottle with a cork.

Jaive and Worabex were dressed untidily. They glowed beautifully.

"Are you rested?" asked Jaive.

"Yes. Thank you, Mother. In fact—"

"Because we have a new project," said Jaive, "and I think it will be of interest to you."

She sat down and the purple kittens climbed up and played in her lap. Worabex inspected the bottle. "It's bubbling Gascain," he told Tanaquil. "I think you'll have drunk it with Lizra."

"Yes."

"To celebrate," he announced.

"To celebrate what?" They leered at each other, the

mage and her mother. Tanaquil arranged her face. "You're going to marry."

They said they were.

Tanaquil told them she hoped they would be happy.

Following that, the meal went, not with a swing, but with a series of lurches.

Sometimes even the dainty demons spilled things, or forgot things. They must have been infected by the general high spirits.

"Do you remember," said Jaive, as Worabex opened the third bottle of wine—the Gascain was still chilling—"how I made the desert seem to bloom, when you were a child?"

"Yes, Mother. It was a very quaint illusion."

"Now," said Jaive, "with my—with dear Worabex's help, we'll do it properly."

"The desert turned into a garden," said Worabex.

"Like my life," fluted Jaive.

One of the demons dropped a dish of gooey sweets. They rolled messily all over the floor.

Jaive looked about vaguely. "You know," she murmured, "I still can't find my flying carpet." She lowered her voice and said to Tanaquil, "Some of the demons have grown skittish. They may have stolen it."

"Yes, I expect so," said Tanaquil, picturing the peeve nest.

"We'll begin this afternoon," said Worabex. "On the desert, that is. It may be worth watching, even for Tanaquil."

"There's a hidden water source," said Jaive. "Worabex my—he found it. Miles down, of course, but we should have no difficulty—"

"Well, he can do anything," said Tanaquil again before she could stop herself. "Look how handsome he's made himself.

Worabex said, "That isn't really magic, young woman."

Tanaquil lifted her head. "No? Ten years younger and a foot taller—"

"Not exactly, would you say," said Worabex. He looked over Tanaquil at Jaive. "You know, excitement, joy, can do all this, too. I knew I was coming to meet your mother."

Tanaquil frowned.

The peeve had learned the frown from watching. But it did not matter now. The peeve had another peeve to watch instead.

Tanaquil decided, instead of trying to talk to her, after all she would need to write to her mother. Another pompous letter. Because if she said now, *I'm going away again,* Jaive might not even notice.

Had Jaive ever unwrapped the emerald necklace? Worabex must have given her the gold snake, and it was a real one. She was feeding it. Thank heavens the peeve—No.

"Now the bubbling wine is ready," said Worabex. "We'll drink a toast to the garden in the des—"

He had been lifting the bottle from the stream. All at once the pressure of the Gascain inside shot the cork out of the neck. It flew across the room and hit Tanaquil, hard and stinging, on her left temple.

"I'm so sorry," said Worabex. Of course, he would not mean it.

Jaive said, "Shall I make a quick spell to stop the bruise?"

"No, thank you, Mother. It's quite all right. It's a way I can remember this day. The day I got bruised."

Tanaquil stood up.

Worabex looked at her thoughtfully. He said, as if from far off, "Try not to learn from pain, Tanaquil. Try to learn from happiness."

"Well, you know all about that."

The demons were giggling in corners. Acting out how the cork had hit the bad-tempered younger witch on the head.

Tanaquil drank a little of the Gascain, and then left them all. If they saw her go, she was not certain.

Learn from happiness! A chance would be wonderful.

In her boots and divided skirt, Tanaquil stalked over the hot roasted afternoon sand, towards the rock hills.

Why she was going there was really a mystery to her. There would be nothing to see. Except wild peeves, playing. Happy peeves.

And the peeve was happy, and Jaive was happy. And Honj was probably quite happy by now, wed to happy Empress Lizra, adored and rich.

"Darn!" shouted Tanaquil. She added a few other exotic phrases. She told the day what she thought of it, and the throbbing bruise, and Honj, and Jaive, and the peeve. "Tomorrow, *no later,* I'm *off.*"

As she left the fortress, there were glints and colors waving above it. Jaive and Worabex must already be at their sorcery. Now and then a dull rumble sounded from somewhere.

It would be sensible to go. Everything here would soon be in such a muddle.

The little shadows of the afternoon rock hills came over

her. They marched across the sand. And she, under the arch of the open rock, shaped like a bridge, or gate, stood in deep shade.

The shade was cool today, as she had never thought it had been. Up there, she had dug for fossils.

She scuffed the sand with her foot. And down *there*, those magic bones, like crystal from the stars. Nothing now.

She felt better suddenly. A little better. After all she had freed a unicorn. And if Honj was happy, and Jaive and the peeve—well, it was good. She was glad.

If only . . . if only she could be happy too.

There was a long ominous clap of thunder. It began under the ground, half a mile away, and came galloping towards her.

Tanaquil looked back at the fortress.

The dunes were spraying and springing outwards. The air was full of dust and fume. Something was coming up. They had summoned the water source, were bringing it to the surface to make their lavish lovers' garden.

But the pressure of the water, rushed from miles beneath, was like the pressure in the bottle of bubbling wine.

Tanaquil knew in that moment what was about to happen. She knew she had been unwise telling no one she was coming to this spot. She knew she was in terrible danger. She knew—

And then, like a growling, blazing dragon of white and green, a gush of liquid exploded out of the desert, tore upwards, up and up, shining and roaring, and struck the roof of the sky.

As it fell back towards her in a sheet of shattering green

steel, Tanaquil thought clearly, *I should have known better.*
Next: *But I'm invulnerable.*

But then the storm of water reached her, struck her, she felt herself whirling round and round, sand in the sky and sky on the ground, until a green fist punched her under the chin, not hurting her at all, and she fell down and down, through the floor of the world beneath the rock gate, down and down into a very silent, empty nothingness. And surely she had done this before, but—*I dunno,* she heard the rat voice say. *Who care?*

Two

VI

I'm in a garden.

The thought was clear and firm. It came because she could hear bird song and the rustle of trees, smell the freshness of leaves mixed with a damp, mushroomy scent. And flowers.

If Tanaquil opened her eyes, she would see.

She thought, *I'm standing up. I expected I'd be on the ground. I fell down, didn't I?*

And then she thought, *I've fallen through another world gate. From the rock hill.*

She opened her eyes wide.

Greenness flooded them.

It was not a garden, but a forest. A lush and overgrown forest. Around the black and emerald-mossy trunks of the trees twined glossy ivy and spotted creepers, in which were tangled clusters of huge scarlet flowers, their petals spread so far, they seemed about to fly away. The ground was woven with creepers, thick with shrubs, and new trees.

Tall pale red mushrooms with sinister dark freckles rose as high as her knees, her waist.

About twenty steps ahead, the trees broke. They had been felled to make way for a broad road paved with green stone blocks. More scarlet flowers, these shaped like swords and pokers, burned along the verge. And above, high over the treetops, was a wide sunny sky. The sky was the softest apple green, and the clouds in it were transparent. They looked like bubbles.

"Yes," said Tanaquil aloud.

She felt well. She had not hurt herself falling through. But then a wave of alarm poured over her. As on the last occasion, the gate must be—up *there*. And she could not see it. Until she found an exit, she had no way out. And she was alone here, this time. Quite alone.

She stood listening. Not an unfriendly world, surely, for the birds sang musically, and now and then she heard a raspy, funny hoot, perhaps from some sort of odd daylight owl. The forest was unusual, but not in any way she could see repulsive or threatening.

Tanaquil liked the sky. Even the neat road. So well made and green. It looked appealing.

Since she was here, it might be best to explore a little.

She walked towards the road, trying not to tread on the masses of little pink, orange, and red clovers growing in the grass.

Just at the road's edge, Tanaquil hesitated. She could hear another new noise. A rusty rhythmic squeaking. What kind of creature was this?

Tanaquil stationed herself behind a tree.

Then she almost laughed. After all, this sort of thing *had* happened to her twice before. She was nearly used to it.

And now she saw what was coming briskly along the road. It was a wobbly wheelbarrow, pushed by an old woman with a shawl over her head.

Oh splendid. The people here look like people, too. That's a bit of luck. Again, she repressed a laugh.

Then she stepped out on the road, almost boastfully. "Good day."

The old woman cast her a look. "Might be good for you but that isn't to say it's good for everyone."

Tanaquil dismissed this obstreperous remark. Once more, beings in a parallel world spoke the same language that she did, which was obviously fortunate. Though it occurred to her, actually, that maybe in fact this was not true, simply that, having arrived elsewhere *magically*, the very nature of the magic enabled Tanaquil to understand and be understood.

"What a useful wheelbarrow."

"It may look useful to you. That isn't to say it is."

"No, I suppose not."

Tanaquil felt irresponsible and giggly. Ridiculously and literally, she had left all her troubles behind.

"May I walk along with you?"

She thought the woman might reply, You might, but then you might not. But the woman said, "Munphf." Which presumably meant, All right, if you must.

They began to go along the green road through the green forest.

"I'm a stranger here," said Tanaquil recklessly.

"Are you."

"Could you tell me where we're going?"

"Tablonkish."

"Oh, Tablonkish. Of course. That's . . . a village?"

"City. Tweetish is the village. Tweetish and Sweetish."

"Yes, I see."

The wheelbarrow was full of something bumpy, and covered by a thick cloth. On the top balanced, Tanaquil now saw—and smelled—a partly rotten cabbage.

"You're selling cabbages in Tablonkish?" she guessed.

The old woman gave her a withering glance.

"*Cabbage* isn't in fashion."

Puzzled, Tanaquil said, "Then what—"

"Ssh," said the woman rudely.

Tanaquil and she walked on in silence, but for the bird song and the squeaks.

Although there had been absolutely nothing threatening about this region a moment before, Tanaquil now began to notice a strange sort of fragmented shadow, that seemed to keep appearing, vanishing, re-appearing, about fourteen or fifteen trees deep into the left hand forest.

"Is there something—"

"*Ssh.*"

"Ah."

On they walked.

And the shadow—the shadows—kept uneasy pace with them.

Tanaquil, staring at the bumps under the cloth, said, "That looks like—"

"Ssh."

"Why? Anyone, or thing, can hear. This barrow squeaks, you know. Who's following you?"

"*They* are," said the woman.

"And who are they?"

"Ssh."

Tanaquil, who had had enough of this, flipped up a corner of the cloth.

"It *is*. It's—"

"Ssh."

"Nuts," finished Tanaquil, deliberately.

As she did it she felt that perhaps she should not have, and here she was right.

There was a sudden outburst of squeaking, but this time from among the trees. Now it decidedly was an animal, or several animals.

"You pest!" shouted the old woman. She stopped moving. "Can't outrun them," she said. "Might have got there. Cabbage could fool them, put them off the scent. But oh no. You have to go and *say* it."

Out of the left hand forest burst three creatures. They were about the size of large dogs, and running on all fours. They were covered with shaggy, grayish fur, and had eager snouty heads. Black beady eyes, black noses, natty little ears. Now they sat back and raised their black front paws. The three noses twitched.

"Go away!" screeched the old woman. She pulled from the barrow a long stick and waved it.

"What—" said Tanaquil.

"Sqwulfs!" cried the old woman.

And then the three peculiar animals dropped down on all fours again. Baring pointed fangs and giving savage squeakings and awful *pmnerr* sounds, they flung themselves at the barrow.

Tanaquil was knocked over. A great hind paw went in

her stomach and winded her. She saw the old woman flailing with the stick, but she was quickly pushed over too. And then the sqwulfs were in the barrow, throwing out the cloth and the reeking cabbage, rolling and burrowing about in the nuts.

There were small nuts like hazels and walnuts, large ones as big as coconuts, and every size between. The sqwulfs noisily dragged up paws full, cracked the shells with their teeth, chomped and snapped. Bits of shell and nut sprayed off in all directions. Nuts rolled on the road. The sqwulfs trampled and sat on others. Their eyes were reddish with ferocity and enjoyment.

"*Wretched* girl!" wailed the old woman.

"I'm sorry, I didn't—" Tanaquil left off. She and the woman sat on the road amid spilled nuts, watching the sqwulfs greedily feeding.

"Couldn't we . . . ?"

"No. Leave them be. Too late now."

When Tanaquil did get up to try to go nearer the wheelbarrow, one of the sqwulfs menaced her. Its cheeks were stuffed with nuts and it looked idiotic, but very dangerous. After that she did what the old woman had said.

When the feeding frenzy was done (it took about five minutes), the sqwulfs gathered vast quantities of nuts in their long, wolflike mouths, plumped down and, jaws now wedged wide, went springing off into the trees.

The rest of the nuts were in a terrible state, but Tanaquil bent to begin picking them up from the road.

"Leave it," said the old woman again. "Once one pack gets the scent, others come. That rotten cabbage might have kept them off. Then it might not. You said the *word*. They understand it, you know. *Nuts*."

"I *didn't* know. I'm sorry."

"You may be sorry," said the old woman, "or you may not be. It hardly matters."

She went to the barrow and tipped out all the remaining cracked and sat-on nuts to the road.

Then she began to wheel the empty barrow off, the way she had been going.

There seemed to be new shadows in the trees.

Tanaquil hurried after her.

"I really am sorry. Can I do anything?"

"Maybe you can. Maybe you can't."

"You're still going to the city, anyway?"

"Might as well. Nearly there. Then again, perhaps I'm not."

Did everyone here speak in this manner?

The forest ended about half an hour later, the jungly trees thinning out. The sun was westering, mild gold in the apple-skin sky, and flocks of birds flew over, twittering.

Beyond the last trees, the ground rose slowly up, covered in thick grass and mounds of flowers, to an impressive rock. The rock too was green, and from it leapt down a picturesque white waterfall. At the foot of the rock were roofs, with some peaceful smoke rising.

"Tweetish," said the woman. "Sweetish to the east. Or not." She pointed upward. "Tablonkish."

The city crowned the rock, just like a crown. And was crowned in turn by a wonderful gleaming, translucent-looking green building, that seemed carved from a single jewel.

"What is that?"

"Might be the palace."

"It's very beautiful."

"Do you think so. It might be, it might—"

"Not," Tanaquil helped out.

A silver banner fluttered up there, in a gentle late afternoon breeze.

There were some pale pink goats grazing near the village. The old woman wheeled the barrow past them and all the goats stared with wicked gray eyes.

"And what's that?"

"What?"

"That shining?"

"The sea," said the old woman. She seemed to think there was no doubt about that.

From the edge of the village under the rock, you could see the sea properly, like a calm jade mirror, folding away and away to the rim of the green sky.

It really *was* beautiful, all this. Not a perfect world, certainly, but glamorous, survivable?

"The Sulkan died," said the woman, "Sulkan Tandor, that is. Now his daughter rules. Sulkana Liliam."

"Oh, yes," said Tanaquil, interested. Something like a clock seemed to start ticking in her head. Some weird memory . . .

"Then there's the other girl," said the woman. "You might get a glimpse of her, or you might not."

"Mmn."

"Red hair like you. Not that I ever saw her. Or I might have. Princess Tanakil."

Tanaquil turned slowly. She stared at the old woman. "I'm sorry, you said, *what* did you say she was called?"

But the old woman was waving now to the goatherd, showing the barrow empty of nuts. And Tanaquil anyway knew, with a jolt of her heart, precisely the name she had just heard: Tana*kil,* almost, if not exactly, the same name as her own.

VII

After apparently everyone in Tweetish had inspected the empty wheelbarrow, and said various useless or consoling things about coming through the forest-jungle, sqwulfs, and being a female on her own, the old woman took Tanaquil to her nephew's house.

"It's very kind of you, especially since—"

"Might be. Might not be."

The nephew, Domba, let them straight in. His wife was frying aubergines and potatoes for an early supper, but did not seem to mind two extra guests.

"Sqwulfs got the nuts again, eh, Auntie?"

"Might have," said the old woman, "might . . ."

Domba laughed, and led them to the table.

While they ate, Domba explained to Tanaquil, the 'foreigner,' that aubergines were in fashion. "Even Sulkana Lili will be eating these tonight."

"I'd be interested to know," said Tanaquil cautiously, "about the Sulkana."

"She's all right. Very quiet. And brave. It's her sister

who's the problem. Bashing about causing trouble."

"Her sister Tanakil," prompted Tanaquil.

"That's the one."

When they had asked her own name, Tanaquil, inspired, had named herself 'Feather,' for the last bit of her real name.

"My sister's called that," said Domba's wife. "Small world, isn't it?"

"Might be. Might not be."

"And where are you from?" Domba asked Tanaquil, trying to put the stranger at her ease.

"Oh . . . Um."

"Um? That's that town to the far north, isn't it? Where the Sulkana's pet daffodils come from."

Tanaquil decided, if they knew about a place called Um, (with . . . daffo*dils*?) she had better not be from there.

"No, sorry. It's just a shortened name we give it. It's really Umbrella."

"Never heard of that."

Bemused, they ate the aubergines. Tanaquil remembered how Honj had taught the peeve many words, and the peeve had mistakenly thought that *aubergine* was a pretty awful swear word.

"Don't be sad," said Domba. "Homesick, I expect. My friend is going up to the city tomorrow. He'll take you, I daresay. See the sights. He's dropping in later. I'll ask."

Sure enough, in the fading peachy light, Domba's friend knocked on the door and stepped in. He was a strapping young man named Stinx.

Very ironically, a light rain was spangling down outside, and Stinx carried—an umbrella. Tanaquil glanced at it uneasily, and, as he was shutting it, chanced saying, "We don't have those at Um. What a clever idea."

"This? Me old rainshade? Yes, that's useful, that is." However, he then gave her a long, astonished, worried stare.

When the rain ended, warm darkness came. Domba and Stinx sat smoking pipes on the porch, among the climbing vines.

Tanaquil helped Domba's wife, Honey, wash the plates.

"I think Stinx took a shine to you."

"Oh. Really?"

"If you were thinking of staying in these parts, you could do worse. He has a house and some land, and ten goats."

Tanaquil decided to keep quiet. But when she went up to the room where she and the old woman were to sleep that night, she could not resist eavesdropping from the narrow landing, as the two men were on the porch directly below.

They were, however, only saying things, thankfully, about their goats and aubergines, and that the next food-fashion might be tomatoes.

There was no moon, but the sky was alight with blue and silver stars. Then, from the forest below, a group of huge stars began to rise as one. There seemed fifteen or more in the cluster, which had a sort of spiral, flower-like shape. Tanaquil recalled irresistibly the complex star patterns of the Perfect World. But this was very pretty.

While she gazed, she heard Stinx say suddenly, in a hoarse, *loud* whisper, "Here, that girl, that Feather. I hope you've been careful what you've said."

"Why's that, then?"

"Well. She's a dead ringer for the red-haired princess on the rock."

"Get away."

"No, I tell you she is. Yer auntie'd tell you. She's seen Tanakil, too."

"Auntie'd say, 'Might be, might not be.' "

"Well, you take my word for it. I reckon if I take her up tomorrow, I'll find meself involved in court matters."

"Don't then."

"I don't mind. Makes a change from me goats."

Tanaquil crept to the bedroom, the second of the two rooms on the upper floor.

The old woman lay on her mattress under a quilt. Tanaquil thought her asleep, but the old woman said quietly, "If you ask me, you're up to some secret business."

"Me? Oh no."

"Listening at the window. Hear something you didn't like?"

"I might have. I might not."

The old woman grunted. Surprisingly she added, "Don't bother about those nuts. I've tried a hundred ways, and never got any of them through the forest. But if *you* come from anywhere I've ever heard of, I'll eat this quilt."

Tanaquil sat on the other mattress.

"You don't get many strangers here."

"We get hundreds of strangers. None like you."

"You . . . don't think I'm like anyone else, then?"

"Might be," said the old woman. "Might not."

Tanaquil did not think she would be able to relax, but at last she did. By then the flower-coil of stars was in the window. Counting them, she fell asleep.

She dreamed that she had made a fire at the edge of the

forest, and was sprinkling into it the red wine they had drunk with supper. Then she cut her finger, like a true witch, and added a drop of blood.

The fire raced up, and out of it burst the red unicorn.

It ran in circles round and round her, the many stars of this unknown world glittering on the green flickers of its bronzy tail and mane. The horn was dark, but gilded with red.

"Stop still," said Tanaquil. *"Stop."*

But the unicorn ran round and round, and she spun slowly to keep up with it, until she fell over and lay on the grass, and then the unicorn leapt into the sky, and vanished among the stars.

In the morning, Stinx arrived bright and early. He wore an elaborate brown velvet tunic and a belt with a silver buckle; his boots were polished, his shirt crisp. Tanaquil felt untidy and slovenly beside him. But there was no help for that. Honey had lent her a hair brush, and sewn up a tear in her divided skirt that the sqwulf had made when knocking Tanaquil over.

After breakfast, Stinx and Tanaquil walked through Tweetish village, stared and waved at.

"There is one difficulty," Tanaquil said, as they came out on a broad road leading away up the rock, "I don't have any money."

"You were robbed, I expect," said Stinx.

Tanaquil tried to be truthful, even though it always seemed to complicate things. "Well actually, I just stupidly came out without anything. I didn't . . . think I'd come so far."

"I can let you have a few coins."

"No, please. I wasn't asking you for that. It's only I can't pay for anything. Usually I earn my money by mending things. I asked Honey and Domba if there was anything in the house that was broken, but they said there wasn't."

"There'll be plenty to mend up in the city," said Stinx, looking at his clean fingernails. "A lot gets broke, up there."

"Does it?"

"I should say so, meself."

They walked on, and began to ascend by the steep road.

In parts, it changed into flights of steps. Then there were terraces where you could rest. The waterfall fell splashing down, very loud now, so that sometimes Stinx and Tanaquil had to shout at each other to be heard. Dark green willows poured out of the rock. Enormous laurels and bay trees leaned towards the fall. In the droplets hung rainbows, and dragonflies darted about.

Soon there began to be houses, and above, the city wall was now visible. It was a red wall with turrets and towers. The silky silvery banners hung still.

The air smelled washed and vital. Birds flew over. Then the noise of the city began to come down. It was the noise Tanaquil remembered from all cities. A mix of shouts and laughter and argument, of wheels and doors and foorsteps, machineries, trades, movement, life.

The first city she had ever seen had been a city by the sea. The city where she found her sister, Lizra.

From Jaive's knowledge of magical parallel worlds, Tanaquil knew that what seemed to be happening was possible. For here there was a Sulkana called Liliam, or Lili, and her sister Tanakil, who might be Lizra and Tanaquil, their equivalent parallel selves.

It was a mad and yet frightening thought.

Tanaquil still hoped it was not a fact. Of course, she had got to learn. Was that foolish meddling, or some other magical law, compelling her?

Meantime, she must get by as best she could.

Near the wall was a market. Huge gates stood open above, leading into the city, but here all sorts of activity went on. There were carts and stalls loaded with items for sale, wines in tall red or black jars, pens of animals, some quite unusual, for example, the *turquoise* sheep. Bolts of cloth fluttered, books stood in stacks, musical instruments leaned. There were tables and baskets of foodstuff. Tanaquil saw enormous piles of purplish aubergines, selling fast. But seemingly aubergines were 'in fashion.'

The sky was glowingly green.

Stinx led her to an outdoor tavern, and bought her a glass of fruit juice and a large chocolate biscuit. She thanked him, and wondered if this might mean he would anticipate special treatment. Stinx still probably believed she was officially connected to Princess Tanakil.

"This is all so interesting to me, as I'm a *stranger*," said Tanaquil. "I don't know anyone at all."

"Right," said Stinx. He rolled his eyes.

Had he put on his finery because he thought Tanaquil would introduce him to the princess and the Sulkana?

"There's a performing magician," said Tanaquil brightly.

"Lots of those," said Stinx.

They went to see.

The elderly bald man in the long robe reminded her of Worabex at once, because he was so totally unlike him.

"For my next illusion," said the old man, "I will show you a wonderful beast. The very beast that is the device on the banner of our revered princess."

There was some muttering. Tanakil, evidently, inspired little enthusiasm.

The magician clapped his hands, and before him on the rock was lit a little fire. Producing a wine flagon from his sleeve, he poured red wine into the fire, which coughed and flared up, releasing a big plume of smoke.

Everyone was coughing now, including the mage.

"Erk erk—just a little hitch—*erk erk."*

"Useless," said Stinx.

Tanaquil, though, recollected her dream.

"Just let's see. I mean, the princess's banner, what is it?"

"A red unicorn."

The expected chill wormed down the back of Tanaquil's neck.

Yes, the magician had stuck a pin in his finger. He shook a drop of blood into the fire.

Instantly it settled. And slowly up from the flames rose a red animal with a glittering horn.

"Not bad," said Stinx, after all impressed.

The crowd gave mocking cheers.

Tanaquil saw this was not the unicorn of her dream. Indeed not. It was twisting about and wriggling now. It sat down on the fire and sneezed.

The crowd laughed. "That's funny! Yeah, well done."

The magician seemed put out.

Then the unicorn gave an extra wriggle. Its horn fell off,

then its *skin*. With a huge pounce it came walloping out of the fire, scattering bits of flame and smoke and magic, cursing and snorting.

"My goodness," said Tanaquil.

She froze in a combination of horror and delight, as, covered in bizarre melted substances, muck and wine, into her arms there kickingly jumped the peeve.

VIII

Having folded his arms, the elderly magician glared at them. "I tell you, it's *my* property. I made it, I conjured it up."

The rest of the crowd yodelled agreement, or pro-Tanaquil support.

"I can quite understand it seems that way," said Tanaquil, as the peeve licked her face and scratched himself. "But actually . . ."

"I won't have this," declared the magician. "I'll call a guard from the gate. This animal is worth a lot of money."

"No it's not," said Stinx, "it's only a veepe. And it's got fleas, too."

"A *sorcerous* veepe," said the magician. "These are my witnesses. I *made* this animal."

"Rrh," said the peeve, giving him a look. "Wet fire."

The magician seemed astounded, then gratified. "As you hear, it speaks. This proves it to be mine."

Stinx leaned forward. He took the mage by the collar.

"Look, you. She says it's hers. It only barked. I'll give you the price of a goat for it."

The crowd applauded. They said that was fair.

But the magician scowled and pushed Stinx off. "Don't manhandle me or I'll turn you into a pigeon."

"Just try it."

"I shall call a guard!"

Stinx hissed into the magician's ear. Tanaquil heard the name *Tanakil.*

The mage drew back.

"Ah, well, in that case."

"Me friend, here, Feather," said Stinx, "and I, and her veepe, are now going on. Take this. Full goat price. And shut up."

The peeve spat out a small flame, which set the magician's shoe on fire. As he was beating it out, Stinx and Tanaquil walked with dignity away.

"Come quick as," said the peeve. "Got here."

Stinx shot the peeve one look, then concentrated on the road ahead and the gate.

"You were wonderful," said Tanaquil. She hugged the peeve, who struggled, descended her, tearing open her skirt again, and trotted along at her side. "Where I come from," she said to Stinx, "we call these animals peeves."

"Veepes," said Stinx.

"I see. You're a veepe," said Tanaquil to the peeve. He took no notice, still scratching the mage's spell out of his fur.

It—no, *he*—had left their own world, left even his lady love, Adma, and somehow followed Tanaquil into this one. She would have to question him as to how, because that might provide the means to get back. Better to wait for that until they were alone.

As they went in under the gate, one of the guards standing there goggled.

"She looks like the princess!"

Tanaquil lowered her head, letting her hair fall round her face. Although the guards did not stop them, and Stinx made no comment, she began abruptly to see she might soon be in very hot water.

Tablonkish had a scent of its sea, along with all its other smells—new bread, horse manure, perfume—but this sea did not have the same aroma as in Tanaquil's world. It was not fishy, not salty. It smelled more like the bubbling Gascain Worabex had uncorked.

She had asked Stinx if he would mind buying her a large hat. She said the sun was bothering her a little. Really she wanted, particularly after the gate guard, to hide her face and hair. She promised Stinx she would repay him as soon as she could. He said, himself, he didn't want repaying. And the hat he chose was a bit much. Pink straw with lots of red roses and ribbons. Put with the rest of her untidy clothes, Tanaquil thought she probably now looked insane. But she tucked her hair into the hat, and it shaded her face rather well.

"Can't see you in there," joked Stinx.

Perfect.

The city was full of interesting things. In one part there was a race track, and yellow horses with lustrous coats were going through their paces, drawing curious-looking chariots that seemed to be too small. Stinx explained this was only a practice. There was a street that wound up the rock full of cheese makers, and another of carpenters, and another of clock repairers. Seeing these, Tanaquil became downcast. No one would need, or allow, anyone else to mend things here.

There were also public gardens, and here they had tomato sandwiches under some very tall trees. Tanaquil had also noticed no one seemed to eat any meat or fish, though she had seen milk being drunk. And there were, in Cheesemaker Street, plenty of cheeses for sale.

"When you've done," said Stinx, "I'll take you to see home."

"Oh, do you live up here?" asked Tanaquil, rather nervously.

"No, not *home*. *Hoam*. The palace, that's the name. Though some of the nobles pronounce it differently."

"Yes, I'd like to see the palace."

Tanaquil realized, more nervous than before, she might even have to try to get *into* the palace. But undoubtedly it would be more sensible not to—why this compulsion? If she had a parallel self here, all the more reason to return to her own world.

It was nice in the park, though. Sitting on plushy grass, looking at two or three people reading, or some nearby children playing a quiet but intense game.

Stinx had bought the peeve-veepe a nutsteak. The peeve had thanked Stinx, who shrugged, and then ceremoniously 'killed' the steak in a geranium bed. The peeve seemed to enjoy the snack, and afterwards lay sunning himself on the grass, paws in the air.

"You may get to see Tanakil," said Stinx, as they walked

up more steep stairways, now lined with marble statues, towards the top of the rock.

"May I?"

"She comes out on Murra afternoon, when Liliam's busy, to ask if the people want anything. They don't much, from her."

This was a lot of information at once.

"Murra—" said Tanaquil.

"It's Murraday today. Forraday tomorrow. Lost track of time, you have, with travelling, I daresay."

"Oh, yes. Of course. When you say, to see if the people want anything—"

"Settle quarrels, give judgements, that sort of thing. Liliam's busy a lot now anyway, with the wedding due next month."

An awful sensation went through Tanaquil's stomach, which was like the tomato sandwich turning into a ball of wet washing and spinning round very fast.

"Wedding."

"Liliam's wedding."

Tanaquil felt she must ask at once whom Liliam was marrying, and why. And lots of other feverish questions. She could not get one of them out. Because, in her world, Lizra had been going to marry Honj. And it seemed as if, here, the same thing must be going to happen.

Stinx had not noted anything.

"Here y'are."

They had come up on to a very wide highway. On either side of the sloping, rising road, which was paved with green and white, stood tall gilded lamp standards topped by golden dolphins holding lanterns. This was very like Sea

City. At the top of the road, stood the jewelry green palace, which seemed partly transparent, and gleamed like emerald.

"Hoam," said Stinx.

From the roofs floated all the silver banners of Sulkana Liliam.

Directly at the road's centre, across from where Stinx, Tanaquil, and the peeve had stopped, rose a magnificent gilded clock tower, with a complicated clock. Even as they arrived, gold figures, soldiers and monkeys, dancers and bears, began to move around its face, and a sonorous bell rang four times.

"Still two hours wrong," said Stinx without surprise.

Crowds of well-dressed people were idling along the road, and several flower and fruit sellers were seated with their baskets at the road's edge. It had been a tranquil scene, but only for a moment.

No sooner had the clock struck the wrong time, than everyone began to push and scurry to the far sides of the pavement, and the sellers of things lugged their baskets in the same direction, away from the road.

From the palace of Hoam came a brazen fanfare. Two impressive gates rolled slowly open. And then some hundred or so soldiers in burnished mail came hurrying down the road, shouting and waving their arms. This did not seem very military.

As they ran nearer, Tanaquil heard the words of the shout they were all using: "Get back! The princess is coming!"

Tanaquil frowned. And on instinct got the peeve by the scruff and hauled him up in her arms.

"No, want—"

"Keep still. Or I'll put you in this hat."

Cowed, the peeve stopped struggling.

Next minute, out of the palace gates erupted a chariot drawn by two leaping, careering, crazy-looking horses. It tore down the road at a quite unsuitable pace, and you saw it had been *very* sensible to get completely out of its way.

The rider of the chariot was a girl dressed in a gold-embroidered gown. A circlet of green gems flashed on her long, unruly red hair, in which, too, there seemed to be tied green ribbons.

As she drew level with the clock tower, she swerved the chariot madly. The horses puffed and pranced. There was a screech and a clatter, and next instant one of the chariot wheels came off and rolled violently into the crowd, which gave way, swearing and laughing.

Somehow the girl in the chariot did not fall out. She slid down on to her feet and stood there glowering.

All noise ceased.

From among the soldiers stepped an extremely elegant and handsome black man, who, judging by his battle decorations and goldwork, was at least a commander.

"Three cheers for the Princess Tanakil," said this man, with a face so blank and a voice so expressionless, he could only be on the verge of howling laughter himself.

The crowd cheered stupidly loudly, and threw up its hats.

Princess Tanakil snarled. She said furiously, "All right. The wheel came off."

Tanaquil stared until her eyes hurt. Then she blinked. But nothing had changed. It was still her own self standing there, in a red-hot temper.

Me, at my very worst.

Was this funny or terrifying? Unbelievable or amazing? *Mainly it's just plain damn embarrassing.*

The elegant black man, still entirely controlled, announced: "The princess will now hear any problems you may wish to put before her. She asks that you be brief, as she has much business at the palace."

The air bulged, trying not to burst with mirth. You could feel it. Strong as an approaching storm.

And Princess Tanakil glared at them all, making sure no one even smiled.

But just then the clock gave out the most appalling *bon-n-n-g.*

The chariot horses reared and went galloping off down the road, dragging the one-wheeled chariot, until soldiers caught them.

Some of the crowd seemed to be crying into handkerchiefs.

Princess Tanakil clenched her fists.

The commander said, so sternly that even Stinx could not restrain a grunt of choked amusement, "You there. Come forward, sir. About which difficulty do you wish to consult the princess?"

And then Tanaquil saw two soldiers pushing forward the elderly magician from the marketplace. Like the princess, he was red-cheeked and angry. And he and she met each other's aggrieved eyes with obvious relief.

"I've been robbed, your highness."

Tanaquil thought, *This has happened—something like this—before.*

And she pictured, almost two years back, the Artisans'

Guild complaining in the street about her, to Lizra in the chariot under the lamppost.

She should slip away. But the crowd was too large, and all keen to enjoy everything.

"Robbed of what, and by whom?"

Princess Tanakil had, of course, Tanaquil's voice. A little rougher perhaps, no doubt from often shouting.

"Two peasants from the village watched my show, and when I invented an animal, forced it from me and made off with it. It was a talking veepe, worth hundreds of silver blonks. They claimed they knew *you*."

Stinx said, "Now we're for it. But she won't mind, will she? I mean, seeing who you are."

"Who am I supposed to be?" asked Tanaquil.

Stinx seemed exasperatingly happy. He said nothing else.

And now the mage was pointing straight at them.

"There, the thieves. And my veepe, too."

Here we go again. All eyes were on Tanaquil, the peeve, and Stinx.

Tanaquil bowed her head under the heavy hat.

She heard Princess Tanakil say, "Bring them here."

And so, of course, the soldiers were driving them now, out into the roadway, under the broken clock, to a spot about ten paces from the princess.

Tanaquil peered through straw and roses. In fact, Princess Tanakil did not have green ribbons in her hair. Strands of the hair itself were dyed bright green. Why did one immediately think this had happened because of some sort of mistake?

"What have you got to say?" snapped Princess Tanakil.

Stinx said firmly, "It's me friend's veepe. I paid him goat

price for it. What more does the old devil want?"

There was a silence. A *new* silence.

Tanaquil grasped it was caused by all the crowd, all the soldiers, the elegant commander, and the princess herself, squinting at Tanaquil, thinking, But she's just like. . . .

"How dare you stand in front of me in that hat?" said the princess in a hard, hot voice. "Take it off!"

Tanaquil hesitated, and in that moment Stinx, the poor soul, swept the hat from her head, revealing her as if *he* were the mage, and *she* his most successful trick.

"*There,* highness."

Everyone gave a collective gasp.

Overhead came a scratchy, tinny sound, and then a clatter and a tinkle, as both clock hands came off the clock and fell in the road.

Tanaquil raised her head and stared unflinchingly at her double. Tanaquil thought, perhaps irrelevantly, *I must never get angry if I look like that.*

Finally, it was the commander who spoke. "Your orders, madam."

The princess said, in a voice like a sqwulf cracking a nut, "Arrest her."

As the soldiers seized her, and the peeve, trying to bite, was stuffed into a sack, and Stinx, trying to land a rescuing punch, was flattened, Tanaquil realized that yet one more thing was wrong. But it was too late to worry about it.

To the joyous congratulations of the crowd, she was marched up the road to the palace of Hoam.

IX

As she waited in the big room, Tanaquil admired the painted ceiling and the painted pillars. She felt light-headed, and still between laughter and alarm. Certainly her situation did not look very promising. Worse than everything might be what had not happened when the soldiers seized first her, and then the peeve. Since the black unicorn had given them both the gift of invulnerability, no one had been able to attack either of them successfully. It was true, people might sometimes tread on their feet (or tail), collide with them, and so on, by *accident*. But deliberately to rush at and aggressively grab them; that should have been out of the question. Yet it had occurred. At the palace, Tanaquil's hands had even been tied together behind her back. As for the peeve, he was still rolling and growling in the sack, over there, against a pillar.

The pillars were effective, though. Painted with long-stemmed blue flowers and scarlet leaves. And the ceiling, with gold—were they vultures?—flying over a big red sun.

With a bang the door flew open.

Princess Tanakil prowled into the room.

It was no surprise when the door handle the princess had just touched fell off. With a curse, she kicked the door shut.

"And now you'll tell me who you are, and what your game is," snarled the princess. "You're a spy, aren't you? You're here to learn our secrets."

Tanaquil found it difficult to treat Tanakil seriously, although perhaps she should try.

"I thought I was supposed to tell *you* who I am, not *you* tell *me* who I am."

"What?"

The princess stared at her.

Tanaquil stared back.

"How did you make yourself resemble me? Is it sorcery? Be careful. I am a powerful witch."

"Oh really?" said Tanaquil. "That's jolly." Over by the pillar, the peeve had stopped grumbling and was keeping very still. Tanaquil maybe would be well-advised to be as careful as the princess had warned her to be. She said, "I'm not a spy. I just came . . . on a visit. I agree, we do look *awfully* alike. Funny, isn't it?"

"Funny? *Funny!* Be quiet. Your insolence amazes me. I could have you put to death at once."

"Could you? Why *would* you?"

"Be *quiet*, I said. I must think."

Tanaquil looked at the floor, whose tiles were painted with little green sea waves. They made her dizzy. She looked out of a long window instead, away over the rock to the sea itself.

The princess stopped in midstride.

"What do you call yourself?"

Tanaquil thought. It would be a mistake to offer her real name, and *Feather* somehow was too soft for all this. Inspiration came to her again. "Quill," she announced. The *last* part of her name, all that made it different from Tana*kil*.

"Quill? Like a pen?"

"That's it."

"Why? Do you write a lot? Letters about foreign powers? *Spy* notes . . ."

"I'm *not* a spy. I'm just . . . on holiday."

"Yes, and the sky is *blue*," sneered Tanakil, witheringly.

Tanaquil laughed before she could stop herself.

At that moment, from an inner door, something came slinking, dark and low, into the room.

The princess glanced at it and shouted, "Sit! Sit down."

The arrival halted but did not sit. It was a black peeve, a proper veepe. With big yellow eyes it looked at both redheads. Then it turned and leapt lightly up on to a tall chest. There it draped itself, two paws and a tail hanging over.

"Is that your familiar?" asked Tanaquil, genuinely fascinated.

"Don't ask questions! *I* ask the questions." The princess strode forward now. She glared into Tanaquil's face. "I can *make* you answer. On the other hand, if you're only the simpleton you'd have me believe, I might have a use for you. There must be a use. You're my double. And at this time—"

She stopped, because, between themselves and the window, in the gap of two pillars, a strange red glowing drifted over the floor, like a faint red ghost. The ghost of—

"What's that?"

"I don't know."

"Don't try to work magic on *me*."

Was it the unicorn? The red unicorn of the dreams? Or only sunlight falling oddly, catching some reflection from some red object in the room?

The princess spoke two or three mysterious words. A circle of light like a plate sprang up into the air—and *broke*.

Both young women jumped back to avoid the dropping, clacking bits.

"I meant to do it," said the princess loftily. "A demonstration. As easily as that, I can break you."

Tanaquil could not resist. She leaned over and made a pass across the pieces. She did not know if it would work, since here her expected powers seemed diminished. Besides, normally, she would never have entered into this sort of symbolic magical duel.

However, the broken plate mended instantly, without a scar.

"You, too! You're a witch!"

"I mend things. And you," Tanaquil added thoughtfully, "break them."

The plate of light vanished. The red glow had melted away.

And someone knocked loudly on the outer door.

The princess spun about. As she did so, her hair flew back and Tanaquil saw the princess had a nasty bruise on her left temple.

That's where the cork from the bottle hit me. Tanaquil had forgotten. She touched her own head. It was no longer sore.

It was apparently the princess now who had both the mark and the headache.

"Who's there?" shouted the princess furiously at the door.

"Oynt, madam. Let me in."

The princess strode to the door. There was some awkwardness, since the handle had come off on the inside. Eventually, Oynt used the handle on the outside.

He was a short plump noble in jacket, sleeves and trousers of clashing mauves. "I must warn you, highness. The Sulkana's coming to see you right now, with her counselor."

"All right. Well done, Oynt."

Oynt sprinted out and off up the corridor. The princess pushed the door almost closed and came back to Tanaquil.

"Get into that pillar."

"I beg your pardon?"

"There. It's a fake. It's hollow. Go in and stay in. How you behave may decide your fate."

"Goody."

Princess Tanakil drew herself up. Though slender as Tanaquil, she seemed to swell like an angry frog.

"All right," said Tanaquil. "Look, I'm going in."

The pillar had a tiny doorknob. Tanaquil used it and the fake pillar opened. Inside there was just room for her to stand. And when the princess slammed this door shut, Tanaquil found there was also a small eyehole to look out through.

She's like me, Tanaquil thought, *if I'd been more like my mother. Jaive at her most arrogant and unreasonable.*

The princess, Tanaquil could see, was pacing now.

On its tall chest, the veepe lashed its tail in time to her steps. Tanaquil tried to peer around to see the sack with the peeve, but could not manage it.

Between two pillars she did glimpse something vaporous, red like smoke. But only for a second.

Out in the corridor, a military escort presented swords to the guard at the door.

Here then, was Sulkana Liliam and her counselor. A horrible idea came to Tanaquil: could this counselor be the parallel of the hideous Gasb, who had served Lizra's father?

Then Liliam glided into the room.

Princess Tanakil bobbed a curtsey.

Well, Lizra never asked that of me. Or did she?

But was this the other Lizra?

Tanaquil studied her. The Sulkana was small and slight. She had a cold lovely face. Her dress was icy white and stiff with silver beading. In one hand she carried an ornamental stick, a sort of rod of office. It had a silver and gold unicorn's head. Her eyes were very dark.

Yes, it was Lizra. Lizra at her coldest and most remote, as Tanakil was Tanaquil at her most hot and irritable.

The only thing that had altered was that the hair of Liliam was snow-blonde, almost as pale as her dress.

"Something has happened," said Lizra-Liliam, coolly to her sister. "Will you please tell me what?"

"Nothing," said Tanakil.

"Something," said Liliam. "There are all sorts of rumors. The war with the north has been over for a year, but they're now saying you caught a dangerous spy or assassin."

"No," said Tanakil. "It was just some . . . an actress, dressed up to look like me. An insult. I expect one of my numerous enemies is responsible. I've thrown her in my private dungeon."

"Very well," said Liliam. "If you're quite sure. What do you think, Jharn?"

Behind Liliam, the tall slim figure of the counselor was only dimly to be seen. But he did not seem like Gasb. For one thing, this man's hair was very long, and exceedingly black and shining.

"Well, madam," he said, "perhaps the princess would like me to question this actress. To be on the safe side."

Tanakil turned away from them both. "Perhaps." She now appeared uncertain, yet excited. All at once no longer angry. Her face had softened and for a moment Tanaquil, in the pillar, saw that just as Jaive had declared, at her best Tanaquil's face could look quite beautiful.

But there was something else, apart from this puzzle.

There was something else about the voice of the man Liliam had called Jharn. Something that made Tanaquil too become smoothed yet unsettled. Something that made her heart beat so hard she thought the pillar started to rock about her.

It was just then that the peeve got out of the sack.

Had he eaten a hole? Whatever, there he was, thrashing across Tanaquil's en-pillared line of vision.

The peeve pounced straight by the Sulkana, and hurtled against the long legs of the man called Jharn.

For a minute there was a little confusion as the Sulkana rustled aside—she seemed far too stiff to hurry—Jharn came into full view, warding off the peeve's thrilled leaps and splutters, and the princess gave a squawk.

Then much more spectacular confusion began as the veepe plummeted off its chest and threw itself headlong, spitting and yowling, at the peeve, who willingly met it.

Veepe and peeve tumbled over the floor, over dainty slippers and masculine shoes, over the dizzy green tiles, biting and rending, bushy tails whacking like whips, kicking and honking disgustingly, brown and black fur flying up in clouds.

X

The dungeon was not so pleasant as the pillared room. But for a dungeon, she guessed, it was not too bad.

There was quite a large high window, with bars ornamentally in the shape of lilies. A clean mattress and pillow lay in a corner, and there was a big jar filled with water. The floor had been swept. It smelled of nothing.

Under the window, the peeve sat, washing carefully after the battle.

Once the Sulkana had swept from the room, and her counselor gone after her, the princess called in her guard to prize the two frenzied fighters apart. There had been quite a few bitten fingers and colorful curses before the veepe was tied, scrabbling and gargling, to a pillar, and the peeve cornered. The guards seemed able to do little else with him. Although they told him some of the things they would like to do, which involved large bonfires and small fur coats.

At last Tanaquil came out of the pillar; there was also a knob on the inside. This rather astonished some of the guards. She leashed the peeve using her sash. That brought back memories, none of them fond.

She and the peeve were then taken by a back way, down a back stair, and pushed into the dungeon.

The light had moved across the window since then. The green sky between the bars was tinged rosily at the bottom. She hoped, by now, Stinx was feeling better, wherever he was.

Tanaquil had not said very much to the peeve. She had been lost in her own jumbled thoughts.

Now, the peeve spoke.

"Not Honj."

"No, not really. Not *our* Honj."

Ours. Mine. Not.

The hurt of it was so unbearable she could hardly bear it. She was stunned. Of all the things she had expected, and maybe she should have expected this too, (the talk of marriage) she had not reckoned that her only love would have his parallel self also in this world. Here his hair was black as coal, he dressed like a nobleman, and he was Lord Counselor Jharn, not Prince Honj, captain of the Locusts. But he was still about to marry the ruler, that must be so. To marry Liliam who was Lizra.

And the way Tanakil had changed. Did she love him here as Tanaquil the Mender had loved Honj, under a sky that was blue?

"Because," said the peeve, in an intent voice, "him in here, like us."

"Yes."

"I come in here too, be with you."

"That was very kind. Loyal. That fight was a bit . . . but

anyway, I'm glad you did come. We need to think about it, too, how you got in. There was a gate, wasn't there, under the rock hill? The waterspout must have activated it."

"Not gate," said the peeve. "*In.*"

Tanaquil nodded. "*In* by the gate. Like before."

"Not, not. *In,*" the peeve raised one paw, put it down.

"You can't explain?" said Tanaquil.

"Not got words."

Frustrated, the peeve pretended he had a flea. He went into a flurry and toppled over. Perhaps trying to make her laugh.

She must question the peeve again, when her head was more clear.

She said, randomly, to ease the peeve's embarrassment, "Some of those men wanted to skin you."

"Couldn't. Invunnyrubble."

"Excuse me?"

"Can't touch. Magic."

"Oh yes, but that doesn't work here."

"Does," said the peeve.

Tanaquil recalled faint flashes she had taken for light off the soldiers' mail as they tried to capture the peeve. Was that the invulnerability after all? She raised her eyebrows. "Then how did they put you in that sack?"

"You went with them. Me go too. Not bother."

"I *had* to go. They were able to *make* me go with them. And tie my hands. And shove me in here."

The peeve, one leg lifted behind his head, regarded her musingly. "Ump."

Then he finished his wash, gave her a nod, turned, and ran *straight through the wall.*

She saw him pass into, beyond the stone, head and body, legs, the tail squirreling through last. All gone.

"What?"

She stood in the dungeon of her double, the Princess Tanakil, gawking at the solid stone of the wall, until, presently, and with just as little fuss, the peeve came rather revoltingly, squidging back through again.

"Rrm," said the peeve. "Feel like bread."

"You're hungry?" she asked blankly.

"Wall, wall. Like bread. Go through crumbs."

"How did you *do* that?"

"Do," said the peeve. "You do."

Tanaquil looked from the peeve to the stone wall. From the stone wall to the peeve. "Are you telling me I can walk through a wall?"

"Mupp," said the peeve encouragingly.

Tanaquil's hands had been untied by one of the guard. Now she went to the wall and put her right palm on it.

"How do I—?"

"Just do."

She paused. Mind over matter? If she *thought* she could, she *could.*

"I'll just put my hand through this wall," announced Tanaquil casually. And put her hand through the wall, and her arm, up to the elbow. The peeve was right. The stone felt just like old bread.

When they were both in the corridor, by the outside of the locked dungeon door, Tanaquil hesitated, looking up the back stair.

Was this magic operating simply because they came

from another world? None of them had seemed to have much magic in the hell-world she had entered with Lizra and Honj, Spedbo and Mukk. And in the Perfect World, she and the peeve had only caused harm.

Also, why had she been able to walk through a wall, yet not able to resist capture?

She thought, with dissatisfaction, probably it all depended on what she truly wanted, or thought she could do. She wished to follow her double into the palace of Hoam, so had not allowed her invulnerability to work, which meant she was able, here, even to overcome the magic of the black unicorn! Now she wanted to be free, she was.

What else was possible?

She found out a few heartbeats later.

Steps sounded on the stair.

Tanaquil thought quickly, *All right. If I can be—I'm invisible.*

And when the guard came down, he walked straight past her, only seeing the peeve, who presumably had not bothered to be invisible. "A veepe, eh. You shouldn't be here, old fellow." And the unwise man patted the peeve's head before going on along the corridor and out of sight.

Tanaquil had trouble stopping herself from screaming with laughter. She should be at least startled. She was not.

And where now? What now?

She ran up the stairs, the peeve bounding after her, and both of them reached the upper door.

Tanaquil said to the peeve, "You'd better be invisible too, for now. But *not* to me."

"Surely," said the peeve. He shook himself. She could

still see him quite distinctly. But she would take a bet, no one else would.

They dove through the iron door.

They returned into the apartment of Tanakil, the big, pillared room. To this the back stair led. No one was there. They investigated quietly.

From the pillared room led a bedroom, with fantastic clothes thrown all over the floor and bed. In the ceiling were gold and silver stars, but in one place a slice of pudding had been flung up at them, rather spoiling the effect. The veepe was also asleep on the bed, but it did not wake.

In the bathroom, on the wall, somebody—Tanakil?—had drawn a picture rather well of pure, stiff, silvery Liliam, with a moustache and horns.

There was a final door. It did not give, so Tanaquil passed through, leaving the peeve to eat Tanakil's sandalwood soap.

"She said she was a witch. It's her sorcerium."

The chamber was not large, but packed by stands with glassy globes, ancient books, herbs growing in pots or dried and stored in labelled jars, bowls of powders, antique bones, spells jotted down in chalk on the walls. On a broad table stood a great darkened mirror. It was a sorcerous mirror. To Tanaquil, who had grown up with Jaive, there was no mistaking it. The peeve ran in, pranced about, lost interest, ran out again.

An apparatus with crystal tubes and bulbs had exploded at the table's far end. Splotches of bright green lay about;

the same shade as the strands in Princess Tanakil's hair.

Why did she break things? Why did her spells go wrong? Why was she so full of *rage*?

She loved Jharn-who-was-Honj. And he was going to marry Sulkana Liliam. Did Tanakil need another reason?

Tanaquil thought: *I know how she feels. Yes, I'm sure I'm that angry too. I could have killed Lizra. Honj said he had to stay with her and I thought he had to stay with her. Poor little Lizra, so sad and all alone. But I wanted him and he wanted me. And we said good-bye for ever.*

"Oh *hell*," said Tanaquil. And the last intact glass bulb in the apparatus burst in twenty bits.

As she was staring, she heard a vague sound beyond the room. The peeve suddenly reappeared half in, half out of the closed door, with a bar of soap in his mouth.

"Them back."

Bubbles blew aromatically from his snout.

Tanaquil and the peeve sneaked through the solid door, across the bedroom, and peered invisibly around the bedroom door, out at the pillared room.

Tanakil had just entered. After her walked Honj—no, *Jharn*. He shut the outer door somehow; perhaps they had fixed the door handle.

Handsome, unique, but not unique at all, he stood looking at the princess with the red hair.

She gave a stifled cry. He opened his arms. She went into them, and he held her.

He loves her too.

The same as us.

The peeve blew an enormous scented bubble and loudly burped.

"What was that?" asked Jharn, lifting his head.

"It's only the veepe."

They stepped back from each other. Went on looking into each other's faces. Very clearly, each was, at the moment, all the other one wanted to see.

Now she's with him she's calmer, strong, quiet. Was I like this, with Honj?

"What are we going to do?" said Jharn.

"Why do you ask *me*?"

"Because I'm lost, Tantal. Just lost."

Tantal. A pet name. How much nicer than Tana*kil.*

"She's so selfish," said Tantal-Tanakil.

"Yes. But your father died. You hardly knew him, but she was with him all the time. And then she met me. She wants me to be her father, in a stupid way."

"I know. Oh, Jharn."

"I can't let her down. She was so brave in the war. You know how they tried to invade us but she was there, day and night, doing all the right things. She was so *valiant*. She only wants the best for all of us."

"I hate her."

"I know. Do you want me to tell her I'll leave her? Could she stand it?" He stood now more straight. "She'd probably throw us out. You'd lose everything you have. So would I. But is that what I should do? I will. Only tell me."

Tanakil's eyes blazed. She lost her beauty and went very red. "Why *should* we lose everything? She wants to be Sulkana, *and* have you. I *hate* her, hate her."

They stood, and strangely, turned away from each other.

On the bed among the clothes, Tanakil's veepe had woken. It was snuffing the air suspiciously. If it could not see there were intruders, no doubt it could scent them. Not to mention the soap.

Tanaquil heard her double say, "There is one plan."

She looked back at the couple standing in the pillared room. At the other Honj and Tanaquil.

"What? I'll do anything you say."

He was weaker than Honj. Was he? Perhaps, Jharn had not had such a rough and tumble life.

"I'll kill her," said Tanakil.

"You'll kill . . . No. No, Tantal. You won't."

"It's easy, with the right spell, some herbs. I won't make her suffer. Something kind. She'll sleep and not wake up. And then *I'll* be Sulkana. *I* will. And you can marry *me.*"

They were gazing at each other now. Their eyes burned with horror and possibility.

Tanaquil, watching, felt deadly sick.

And the peeve belched again, and the veepe jumped off the bed.

"Want a bone?" the peeve sweetly asked the veepe.

The veepe looked about, surprised. "Bone want. Me give," said the veepe. Ridiculously it seemed, it too could talk, but backwards.

The peeve turned. Tanaquil saw he had stolen one of the antique bones from the sorcerium. As he thumped the veepe on the nose with it, there was a blinding flash of sorcerous lightning.

Tanaquil, with the practice of years, gripped the peeve

by the scruff, and just like one of her own mother's demons, dragged both of them down through the floor of the bedroom, hopefully into some saner, safer place.

In fact, they landed in a guardroom, in somebody's snack.

Some sort of yogurt dish went flying in all directions and as the three guardsmen started to tell each other their tea had 'gone off' like a 'cannon,' Tanaquil and the peeve scurried invisible to a corner, where only the licking noises of the peeve, removing the yogurt from his fur, caused accusations of mice.

They listened to the guardsmen for about half an hour. Sometimes other guards came in.

They were all talking eventually about some event tomorrow, the Rot-Chair Race on Forraday.

It sounded devastatingly unimportant.

In the end, Tanaquil and the peeve, invisible as air, swam up through the building to a great garden on the palace roof, looking out to sunset and sea.

Here the peeve chased uncatchable moths in the green and rosy evening, and Tanaquil watched that coil of brilliant flowery stars come up, the ones she had observed from Domba's house.

Other people strolled about. None of them saw Tanaquil or the peeve.

She means to kill her sister.

Would Tanaquil ever have—no. No, she never would. Lizra had been dear to her. She had loved Lizra. And yet, that made it worse.

She sat up in the boughs of a tall magnolia tree, and thought, *I have every power in this world it seems that any sor-*

ceress could want. How can I stop her? How can I make it right?

In the end she must have dozed. She woke because a man was sitting under the tree talking to himself. The peeve was sitting in his lap, and he was stroking the peeve. So the peeve was visible, had decided to be.

"To win a race isn't everything," said the man to the peeve.

"Ufp," gobbled the peeve, who was eating a large cake that, perhaps, the man had bought for himself. The man drank from a bottle. He sounded a little drunk. It made Tanaquil—recalling the soldiers—like him.

"Win or lose," said the man, "laughter's the thing. What's in that cake? It smells like sandalwood."

XI

Waking, Tanaquil stretched. And almost fell out of the magnolia. Probably that would not have mattered. She would just have floated lightly to the ground. Then again, if she had not by now realized she could float, who knew?

"What a beautiful morning," said someone below.

Tanaquil looked down through the creamy flowers, and saw the elegant commander, more casually dressed and without his plumed helmet. He leaned on the magnolia, gazing at a lovely black girl. "But, Velvet," said the commander, "I'm worried about him."

"You always worry about your friends," said the girl. His hair was tight, crisp and curly. Hers gleamed and reached the ground.

"Jharn is so . . ." the commander made a gesture. "He's unhappy, he's angry. He won't say why. He shouldn't marry the Sulkana."

"No," said Velvet. "But you *mustn't* tell him."

Tanaquil spied the peeve, emerging from a bush. The

peeve sidled over to Velvet, and put a paw on her skirt. He had a red flower in his mouth, and his most extreme cute look.

"The flower's for you, I think," said the commander.

"Is it? For me? *Thank* you. Aren't you a sweetie. Whose veepe are you?"

The peeve modestly kept quiet and bounded off. This sickening fawning, though, Tanaquil remembered how the peeve had been with Lizra. Maybe it—he—just had a flirtatious streak.

"I'm hungry, Rorlwae," said Velvet.

They went, arm in arm, across the garden. It was so easy. To be in love, to be together.

Tanaquil frowned. She slid down the tree, scraping her ankle, when she knew she could have floated.

She, at least, was still invisible. She passed two gardeners, one of whom flung a shovel of dirt all over her. When she reached a slender fountain, she lifted the handy brass cup to her mouth and drank. A small boy, who had been watering the path, saw the cup, sailing up and down by itself, or so it looked, and rushed into the shrubbery calling and waving his arms. She needed to be more careful.

What am I to do?

She must go in and find the princess. She must talk to the princess. It came to Tanaquil that by now somebody might have noticed her escape from the dungeon.

She turned and shouted across the early morning lawns of the roof garden: "Peeve! *Peeve!*"

When he came, he had been garlanded with orange daisies by someone, and in his mouth he now held a large

slab of new bread filled with fruit. They divided this by the
fountain.

"I'm going to have to see the princess."

"Gone to race," said the peeve.

"How do you know?"

"Heard it."

"What *is* this race, anyway?"

The peeve looked at her. He said, innocently, "Chairs."

Through a gap in the foliage, an enormous yellow croc-
odile pushed its way, closely followed by two more.

Tanaquil sat absolutely still, holding the peeve in a vise
of steel.

The crocodiles' mouths, as they waddled by, were lined
with sharp, awful teeth. They ambled among the bushes.
From the frightful mouths, long thin tongues darted out,
and slipped gently into the hearts of flowers.

"Suck nectar," said the peeve. "Daffodils."

"But the teeth . . ."

"Don't use teeth."

Tanaquil sat in wonderment. The peeve ran off again
and played round the daffodiles, which grumbled faintly,
showering him with spilled pollen, lumbering over him,
sharing the bushes with the early bees.

It did seem most of Tablonkish was going to the Rot-Chair
Race.

Tanaquil recalled where the race track had been, but it
would hardly have mattered if she had forgotten. Chariots and crowds on foot were streaming along the main
roads. Many wore ribbons or sashes or even flowers in a

selection of bright colors, undoubtedly the racing colors of various competitors.

There was an air of festivity and good humour that Tanaquil felt unsuitable. Nobody else knew that the city's princess had murder in her heart. Nobody knew the cold prim little Sulkana was the cause of such hatred.

Tanaquil was jostled, and the peeve was trodden on. In the end she pulled him aside into an alley.

"Listen, I don't like this."

"No," agreed the peeve.

"I mean I don't like the fact I can't be seen. I keep hearing private conversations. It was bad enough being able to overhear what Tanakil said."

"Rrp."

Tanaquil explained her notion to the peeve. "I don't even know if it will work. But everything else has, here. I don't know why."

"It's you," said the peeve.

"No, it can't be. I've never been able to make myself invisible before. Or pass through solid walls on my own. Anyway. Let's see."

She shut her eyes, and visualized herself, clearly to be seen, but in a quite different form. When she opened her eyes she gave a faint scream.

"It's *me*," she said to the peeve.

"It's you," said the peeve.

"Don't scratch that collar," she added quickly. Now on show again, the peeve had a (magicked up) collar of silver set with large topazes.

"Itch!"

"It can't, it's only an illusion."

However, the sky green silk dress she had invented for herself felt real enough and whispered as she moved. It was embroidered with blue beetles.

Tanaquil turned, and in a glass window at the alley's end, she caught a glimpse of her new self.

She was fairly imposing. A large handsome woman, with thick black hair in an ornate style, and holding a proper ladylike sunshade.

Tanaquil had always rather admired large women, perhaps a supressed admiration of her mother . . .

"You must walk to heel. Please."

The peeve pattered to her side. She hoped it would stay helpful.

Now I'm a shapechanger, just like Worabex.

When they joined the crowd once more, people gave way in respect. Men stepped gallantly aside. Children goggled. She now heard her clothes discussed, and who she might be.

Eventually, at the gate to the race course, an usher asked politely for Tanaquil's ticket.

"Wretched servant lost it," cried Tanaquil in a plummy ringing voice. "Sent him home, of course."

"Well, of course, but you see . . ."

"Ah, there's Oynt," declaimed Tanaquil, seeing the princess's fat little noble spy, riding up in an open carriage. Today he wore three shades of clashing, sicky green, with an enamel pocketwatch, and a knot of extra-clashing red ribbons for the race. "Oynt, my dear man. Please explain to this person I must come in with you."

Tanaquil loomed like a ship's figurehead. She felt herself doing it. Oynt, looking flustered, annoyed, but also flattered, jumped down and came capering over. "It's Lady, er, Lady . . ."

"Feather," boomed Tanaquil, using her other false name. She rapped him playfully with a feather fan she had conjured up. Oynt simpered, and flapping his own ticket to the Race, escorted her proudly through the gate and up the terrace to the best seats, all the while his head on a level with her shoulder, and the peeve skipping behind, eyeing Oynt's puke-shade tasselled shoes greedily.

"In my town of Umbrella, we don't have this race."

"Oh, no. It's unique to Tablonkish. The former Sulkan, Tandor, didn't care for it, said it was undignified."

"But the Sulkana allows it."

"The Sulkana Liliam has everyone's best interests at heart. And here she is!"

Trumpets were sounding over the course. Everybody rose.

Just below their cushioned seats was a silver throne with a silver banner planted behind it. Tanaquil had noted that Liliam's emblem was a silvery unicorn's head. Next to the throne was a chair with another banner, a red unicorn, head and body, the device of Princess Tanakil.

Down the steps came slowly the very dignified—her father's daughter still—Liliam. She wore dark grey and gold. Not a single racing color. (You imagined her saying, "I must show no special favors.") She might have been made of packed snow, a snow-woman, but one made by a professional adult artisan who never smiled.

Had Lizra been as cold as this? Not at first. Later. *Had* she?

Behind the Sulkana and her attendants walked the red-haired princess. Tanakil looked pale and awkward, and one of her fingers was bandaged. Tanaquil sensed that Tanakil was rarely seen without some cut or bruise, and even as she looked at her and thought this, a string of pearls round the princess's neck, broke, and scattered them all over the steps. There were smothered titters, and the servants scurried to pick up.

In the middle of this, Counselor Jharn walked down the steps, straight past Tanakil, and took the Sulkana to her throne.

He too looked pale, and set. His resemblance to Honj made Tanaquil's heart twang like a harp string badly played.

But she was Lady Feather now, and Oynt was offering her chocolate-covered orange slices and raisin tea.

The peeve sat on Tanaquil's lap, so well-behaved and brushed-looking, she was distinctly uneasy.

Instead, it was the princess's black veepe which was chasing pearls all over the steps, barking. Its leash, of course, had snapped.

When everyone was finally seated, a herald strode out on the race track and, reading through a gilded megaphone, informed the crowd of the names of the racers.

Tanaquil did not really concentrate on this. She was watching the royal party just below her. But nothing seemed to be going on, and though there were drinks and sweets, Liliam declined them all, and Tanakil was nervously eating and drinking them, and spilling things.

Tanaquil was acutely aware of Tanakil's words about poisons, herbs, not waking up. This last, however, implied the bane might not be given her sister until the evening. Also she would surely need space and time to prepare the fatal draft, a lot of space and time, given her incompetence.

"Try these strawberry candies from Sweetish," said Oynt. "The Princess likes them."

Now anyway, the racers were riding out, and the crowd was cheering, brandishing flags, and stamping.

"There's my man," declared Oynt. "Fnim son of Phnom. A noble, but got no money, lives in a hut."

"What—what are they *riding* in?" asked Tanaquil-Feather with her most Jaivesque imperiousness.

"That's it, you see. Not a chariot. Each man drives in a rotten chair, on wheels."

"But that's absurd."

"Oh yes. It's traditional."

"Isn't it dangerous?"

"I'll say. Look, they're lining up now."

Tanaquil watched in amazement.

At the starting line directly below she could now clearly see, and add up, twenty-seven racers.

Each man, or woman, of whom there were seven, wore the bright color of one of the ribbons or sashes the crowd had on. Also a sort of leather body armor, boots, and helmet. Each person was firmly strapped into a huge grotesque chair. Some appeared to be made of ebony or mahogany, a dozen had goldwork, and a couple seemed to be solid gold *thrones*. Some had bits missing. Others leaned to one side.

Under each chair was a sort of axle and four wheels, and

a yoke-pole ran out to a pair of horses standing side by side, polished yellow as plums, or dark yellow, like laburnum, or faded yellow as old paper.

All the horses seemed rather too energetic, kicking and plunging and shaking their heads, each of which had plumes to match the racer's color.

"Why *rotten* chairs? Or are they?"

"Partly. They have to be past their best or they can't enter. It makes for better sport."

"Oh, I *see*. And the horses are all mad."

"They feed them on grain soaked in wine. The horses are a bit drunk."

Tanaquil frowned. Thought better of it. She was Lady Feather now. She slapped Oynt quite painfully on the wrist with her fan. "Excellent."

Just then the herald waved a flag from the side of the track. The crowd, everyone, townspeople and nobility alike, not the Sulkana perhaps, began to count.

"*One. Two. Three . . .*

"*GO!*"

And the race was on.

"There he goes! There goes Fnim!"

"Lovely," said Lady Feather. "The one in bright red?"

"That's him. The chair's been in the family for two hundred years. Oak with gold rosettes. Got woodworm. He always races. Always overturns. Broke his leg last year. Fnim's drunk too."

The peeve was standing up on Tanaquil's lap. He looked interested. Gaping after the racers, who were now whirling and bucketing down the track at a reckless speed, she thought she recognized red-clad Fnim. He was the man who had sat under the magnolia and given the peeve his cake last night.

When the track curved to the right for the first bend, three of the chairs toppled over. The back came off one, another lost its wheels and axle, the third ended upside down. The horses jumped and bellowed, and grooms came running from the side of the terraces to drag them away. The upset racers crawled out as best they could, shaking their fists.

Twenty-two rot-chairs careered onward, one of them being Fnim's.

Some of the riders were quite elderly, at least two had long gray beards. Fnim, as Tanaquil recalled him, was about thirty, slim, but lazy-looking. He had had a sad, humorous face.

Oynt was standing up now, as the racers bundled rowdily round the next bend, and went by below their section.

"How many laps?" Tanaquil asked.

"Lots," said the peeve, approvingly.

Tanaquil slapped him weightlessly. "Not that sort of lap, not to *sit* on. I mean how many times round the course."

"Oh, does it talk?" asked Oynt vaguely. "Just like the princess's veepe. You must be a witch, my lady."

"I just dabble, you know," said Lady Feather.

"It's only five laps," said Oynt. He gave a yell as Fnim son of Phnom nearly collided with one of the graybeards. They slid dramatically into a group of four other chairs, all of which went over, and one of which—the second graybeard's—exploded in bits. This graybeard had no ideas of leaving the course. He cut the straps holding him to the remains of the chair, leapt on one of his horses, and was off down the track howling.

"Disqualified," said Oynt, damningly. "But you see, Fnim's still in his chair. He puts a special raspberry poultice on it, you know, just before the race. Makes the woodworm sleepy."

"How quaint."

In the front line of the royals, gorgeous Commander Rorlwae, dressed to the hilt, was slapping the air and shouting. He too wore a red ribbon. Velvet wore an entire red dress and she too was waving, a small brown cat with a red ribbon on its tail, meowing from her shoulder.

Though poor and hut-dwelling, Fnim must be popular with the court.

Now the graybeard on the yellow horse dashed by beneath. The crowd cheered and jeered him. Next came the remaining twenty chairs. Fnim was placed sixth.

"Come on, Fnim son of Phnom!" shouted Oynt, Rorlwae, Velvet. Even Jharn stood up and shouted. He looked happy for a moment. Tanaquil quaked.

As he went by, Fnim lifted a graceful hand, and nearly lost control of his horses.

By now there was a lot of wreckage on the track—three more chairs had gone, one breaking in half—and although the horses were led off, the wrecks were left where they happened, creating obstacles.

Tanaquil watched everything in an astonished blur, standing up now, as everyone except the Sulkana and the princess seemed to be, the peeve round her neck and leaning out like a snake.

At every turn, chairs crashed into each other or simply

collapsed. Two more aggrieved riders were galloping about the course on their horses, one a woman with horse-yellow hair, going the wrong way.

The whole thing was chaos.

And in the midst of her muddled, tickled horror, Tanaquil thought, *Just like everything else.* Was this what life was, a mad race full of accidents and spills, the need to win or at least survive, the likelihood of going over, and all of it strapped in a chair that was magnificent but *rotten*?

Smash-bash. Two chairs turned somersaults. Their four horses, bucking free, went thrashing off at top speed. Another chair went into the back of the other two. These horses were presently standing on the fallen chairs, with furious grazed human faces peering between their legs.

The yellow-haired woman went pounding past again on her horse, the wrong way, a groom hobbling after her yelling "Lady Wombat, *please* get down . . ."

The course was now littered with multiple wrecks and stray galloping horses. It was apparently the fifth lap—Tanaquil had lost track entirely—and there were ten chairs left. Fnim was running second.

"Come on, Fnim! *Comeonfnim!*"

As they approached, Fnim drew suddenly into the lead.

A white ribbon had been lowered, showing the finishing line, directly under Liliam's throne.

The previously leading chair, with a man in bright blue, was now not quite neck and neck with Fnim.

They had perhaps ten yards to go. The blue man abruptly craned over, pulling something from his leathers, throwing it—it was a black cloak—directly over Fnim's head.

Fnim, the chair, disappeared in the cloak.

The terraces shrieked.

"Foul! Foul!" squalled Oynt.

The air was loud with curses.

Fnim's chair, inky-wrapped, spun over and went down. The horses dragged it. But the blue man who had cheated rode into the finishing ribbon.

"Disqualified!" screamed a thousand voices.

Tanaquil saw that the Sulkana was on her feet. She was at the barrier, leaning over.

For a moment, even seen from the back, Liliam looked like a little girl.

Jharn had gone to her. Tanaquil heard him say, "He's all right, Lili. The horses have stopped. Look, he's getting up."

"Fnim's family to her, you know," said Oynt to Lady Feather. "Fnim's third-cousin-removed to Lili."

Fnim, flourishing the cloak, stood under the barrier, grinning like a clever clown who had meant to do it all.

It was Rorlwae who leaped over the barrier and seized Fnim's hand.

As the last chair racketed in to the finish, Rorlwae raised Fnim's arm high.

"The winner!"

The crowd bawled. Oynt kissed Tanaquil's (Lady Feather's) hand. Oh dear. Apparently he was getting a thing about Lady Feather.

Through it all, Tanaquil saw Princess Tanakil had risen and was offering Liliam a goblet of reviving drink. Which after all might not be what it seemed.

"Peeve! Go knock that cup *over*!"

The peeve did not argue.

With exquisite agility he sprang, knocked the goblet flying all over Tanakil's dress, and landed smack on top of the black veepe. Veepe and peeve resumed their battle with cheerily consenting violence.

XII

And so, if life was a Rot-Chair Race, you could lose and still win.

As Lady Feather was riding back to the palace of Hoam, (Or *Harm,* as she had discovered most of the nobles called it) in Oynt's open carriage, a guard rode up and saluted.

"What is it, Werp?"

"Lord Oynt, there's been a little difficulty."

"Excuse me," said Oynt. He stopped the carriage and walked to the side of the highway with Werp.

Tanaquil looked at them. A pity she could not hear from this distance, and over the noises of the passing crowd, what they said.

At once, she found she could hear. She heard Werp and Oynt as clearly as if she stood between them.

"And so we didn't take her any supper, but went down this morning, quite late, because of having a bet on the race."

"Yes?" asked Oynt impatiently.

"And the dungeon was *bare.*"

"You mean she'd got *out*?"

"Yes. The spy-assassin *and* her nasty biting animal. Both gone. And the door locked fast and the bars still on the window. We said before, but we were sure then. A *sorceress*."

"Have you told the princess?" asked Oynt.

"We thought . . . you might . . . break it to her."

Oynt pulled a face.

When he came back to the carriage he was plainly worried. But Tanaquil, aided by her ridiculous magical powers, did not need to wheedle his worry out of him. Sorceress indeed.

The peeve, full of satisfaction, was asleep at her feet. Once again separated from the veepe, he seemed quite happy to come quietly. Tanaquil-Feather, grandly bowing to the Sulkana, had carried the peeve away. The veepe who, this time, had bitten Rorlwae and three guardsmen, was still a sizzling, cursing mass of fur and fangs, barely held by Princess Tanakil. And Tanakil was herself covered in honeyed wine that might have been poisoned. She glared at Lady Feather. But she seemed not to recognize the peeve either. All veepes, apparently, at least according to angry and bleeding Rorlwae, were the same.

Jharn had been congratulating Fnim, and taken little notice. Liliam herself had given Fnim her own clean white hanky to wipe off the dust, before she crowned him with the winner's garland.

When they reached Hoam or Harm, Oynt escorted Tanaquil-Feather up flights of marble stairs, and into an elaborate banquet hall. There was a huge fish tank set in the ceiling above, and Tanaquil, glancing up, was surprised to see large white gulls busily swimming or flying about in it. She made no comment on this to Oynt.

Although the Winner's Feast was very impressive, with endless dishes and wines, it went on, by tradition, from noon until Rose-rise—whatever that was. Tanaquil was soon bored and exasperated. She wanted to take the princess aside, get her alone, and there was no chance of that. Tanakil, in a new unsplashed dress, would presumably preside over the whole feast, with her sister. Jharn sat between them, too, and Tanakil's face had become beautiful again. It seemed she was in no hurry to rush off. Oynt meanwhile had obviously decided he would tell her of her double's escape later. *Much* later.

Instead he plied Lady Feather with food, (he was chirpy again with wine) and liquid.

Snatches of conversation, and Oynt's monologue droned round her like large flies.

"Magic is running wild. This boy saw a cup diving about by itself—" "—The guard had yogurt thrown at them by a demon!—" "Do you know I write poetry? For example, Lady Feather, your eyes so sweet, just like a sheep—" (surely she had misheard?) "—And someone has seen a unicorn red as rust, red as the princess's hair—"

When Tanaquil woke with a slight start, the light in the windows was much deeper, the bubbly clouds tinged pink. What had she been dreaming? Sweet sheep and the *unicorn*.

"Ah," said Oynt, "I do so value it, you know. A friend who's a good listener. I know you felt every word, the way you kept so still, with your eyes shut. *Picturing* it all." He was giving Lady Feather his most sugary gaze. "And how I admire your hair. You know, it even has a glint of red in it, in this light."

Tanaquil nervously checked her disguise. But nothing else seemed to have faltered even though she slept.

The peeve was now, however, standing on the table. A large silver dish had been brought in, smoking, of—as Oynt told her—fashionable aubergines fried in oil, with herbs.

Everyone was greeting the dish, praising the aubergines. The peeve seemed shocked, offended.

"No, no," he prattled, "*not* say word in polite company. Say *muttok*!"

But muttok was the true swear word with which the peeve had confused aubergine. And apparently muttok was known here, for Oynt gasped and raised his brows.

"How naughty, Lady Feather. How daring. To teach it to say *that.*"

As the servants served the guests with aubergines, (how did they have room?) she saw Fnim laughing. He was sitting at the Sulkana's right. Liliam was laughing too. Then Princess Tanakil was being handed a dish. On it was a big cooked tomato, and Tanakil was adding seasoning from lots of little silver shakers. Tanaquil also saw that the princess wore a large silver ring.

In how many stories did someone carry poison in a ring and let drop one drip upon some food, unseen?

"What is the princess doing?"

"Oh," said Oynt, irritated at being interrupted in further talk of his poetic self, "it's the Victory Treat for the Race Winner. He and the Sulkana share it, alone. And the princess always prepares it. The next about-to-be-fashionable vegetable."

And it was almost evening too. Careful poison, one drip, to make Liliam sleep and *not wake up*.

Lady Feather—Tanaquil—jumped to her feet.

Many of the guests were standing, moving about. No one noticed. The peeve was creeping towards the aubergines, loudly muttering *Muttok*.

And Princess Tanakil had given the dish of tomato to a servant, who was presenting it to Liliam and Fnim.

He too was to be a casualty. How heartless and careless frustration had made Tanakil.

The Sulkana was pledging Fnim.

The guests were applauding the soon-to-be-fashionable tomato, which was bursting with chopped nuts and cheese.

Fnim and Lili raised their silver forks.

Lady Feather threw her feather fan as hard as she could. It landed splat in the tomato, which burst, covering Liliam and Fnim son of Phnom from head to lap in nuts, cheese, pips, and red juice.

Astonished and accusing, Liliam's court turned to Tanaquil. Some of the guards had hands on their dress swords. Rorlwae was scowling.

"Good luck!" shouted Lady Feather. She stood there, full of merry kindness, beaming.

Even Jharn was looking at her, although she could suddenly see the corner of his mouth flickering.

"Old custom, you know," roared Lady Feather. "Wish the winner fortune. And the Sulkana, of course. At Umbrella, we throw them—tomatoes, that is—at launched ships. At the prince, too. Oh you should see him sometimes, covered in 'em."

Jharn made a choking sound. He put his hand over his face. He shook. Rorlwae was now doing the same.

Velvet managed, "Well, we'll just have to fetch another tomato."

Fnim (quite serious?), rose and bowed to Lady Feather.

Servants were mopping the Sulkana.

But Princess Tanakil's face was so furious that Tanaquil almost quailed.

"Who are you?" demanded Tanakil.

"Feather of Umbrella," said Tanaquil.

The peeve had reached the aubergines and slapped the dish with a paw. *"Muttok."*

Those who heard were stunned into silence.

Tanaquil was aware of an order for a new tomato being given, but Oynt was now drawing her away from the table. She had no excuse not to go. The peeve, turning sternly, came after them.

I should have watched her. I must *watch her.*

A terrace ran out from the banquet hall. One could see across the roof garden to the sea. A beautiful, a peaceful view.

And from the sea, the glorious sparkling flower-knot of stars was rising. Surely it never rose in the same place twice . . . which was just like the hideous moon of the hell world. This seemed odd, mixed up, like everything else.

But Oynt was pointing.

"Isn't it a romantic light, Lady Feather? The Rose. Now it's risen, the Winner's Feast ends. We can do just what we like."

The Rose. The stars were called the Rose.

But it was *"The tomato!"* she heard inside the room.

Tanaquil caught the peeve to her, thrusting Oynt, surprised, away.

"You must do it again. Do you see? *Tomato.*"

"Muttok."

"No, you fool. Look, there's that bad veepe on the table. Go and fight the veepe again and knock the tomato off the plate."

The peeve looked at her. "Not polite."

Oh God, at this moment, as once more Tanakil sprinkled her killer's potion, the peeve chose to get stupid ideas about social behavior.

And then she thought, *But I can do anything here. As Oynt said, we can do just what we like.*

She stared across the room. No one could even blame her now. She willed the tomato off the plate, and there it went, soaring high, splashing down on the bad black veepe. She had not meant that to happen—

There were screams. "Wild magic" "I told you" And presently worse screams.

The peeve, better late than never, was sprinting back to the table. Landing in the aubergines, it skidded for several feet, fetched up by the veepe, and pulled it over among the fried vegetables.

Now they were fighting for the squashy tomato. *Why?* And if it were poisoned . . .

But the princess was rising like a red star of fury. She raised her arms above her head in rage and there was an awful crack.

Above, the ceiling tank broke open, green salt water

poured upon the guests, the gracious table, the luxurious leftovers, and out flew sixteen seagulls, flapping and squawking and dropping unwelcome little wet presents on the heads of one and all.

So ended the Winner's Feast.

Oynt clutched Lady Feather to him. "Dear Feather, I'll protect you. You've become very dear to me, dear Feather. . . ."

But Tanaquil pulled away and left him, pretending that she did not know what Oynt meant.

XIII

No sooner had Tanaquil reached an alcove off the banquet hall, than she threw off her shapechange. She made herself again invisible. It was a vast relief. Only then did she call the peeve. Who, to her enormous astoundment, came charging up to her.

"*Be invisible too.* Right. Did you eat any tomato?"

"Not poison," said the peeve.

"How do you know?"

"Know, just."

"Don't talk backwards like that veepe. Did the veepe eat any?"

"Not important. *Not* poison."

"Wait," Tanaquil gathered her wits. "You knew I thought it was."

"She not done it yet. Scared."

"Again, how do you know?"

The peeve, which to her was visible, *shrugged*. It actually did so. "In," said the peeve. "You."

"What do you mean?" The peeve scratched. It was em-

barrassed, and had aubergine and tomato pips in its fur.
She stroked its head lovingly. Had it come to harm?
(Harm-Hoam) "If you feel at all funny, tell me."

"Funny? Joke?"

"No. Sick or unwell."

The peeve winked at her. "Muttok bad. Aubergine is vegetable?"

"Yes. You got muddled. But it's like that, here."

Through a window, the Rose . . . rose. Stars. Jharn. Honj.

"Why did you go after the tomato, after I'd—"

The peeve said, very clearly, "Do anything here. Felt
like it."

"Oh. All right. We'll leave it. I have to find the princess.
She left when I did. *Swept* out. Let's try her apartment."

"Go up through floor?" asked the peeve eagerly.

"Yes." She picked him up. "Hold tight."

Like the star-Rose, they rose.

Tanaquil was thinking of what she had seemed to hear at
the feast. The praise for Liliam. About a war, when they
had been invaded, and Lili had ridden out on a primrose-
colored horse, along the lines of the army, under the banner of the silver unicorn's head. She had encouraged her
soldiers, Take no notice of the enemy cannon. She had
helped them all. Her father, the Princess Tanaquil's father
too, Tandor, had been cold and unkind. But Sulkana Liliam put her people first. And if she had chosen Jharn as
her husband, because he was brave and handsome and
strong, she should have him.

The peeve had not really reacted to Tanakil. Surely the

peeve should have been confused between Tanakil and Tanaquil, worse than over the aubergines.

Anyway, they had now risen into the rooms of the princess. Who was not there.

"I know," said Tanaquil to the peeve, who was giving signs of seeking the soap in the bathroom again, "her sorcerium. The mirror. That might show me where she is."

In the sorcerium of Tanakil there was no evidence of poison-making. Everything was as before. The mirror loomed on the table. It was dark as an eclipse of the moon.

If I can do anything here . . .

"Mirror, mirror," said Tanaquil. She waited. The mirror cleared. Now it was like a silvery sheet of ice on a strangely vertical lake.

She had better test it. How?

"Show me the goat owner, Stinx," said Tanaquil.

Colors rippled through the mirror. It settled. A scene appeared. It was Domba's house in the village of Tweetish. Stinx was lying in a hammock, fanned by a girl with long brown hair. Honey, Domba, and two goats were fussing round him. While the rest of the village seemed crowded to the porch, hanging on Stinx's every word. The mirror gave no sound, but Stinx looked very well and utterly smug. The unpleasantness with the Princess's soldiers and his lost hopes of Tanaquil's introduction at the palace seemed to have done him no harm. Tanaquil was glad. Wishing to repay him for the food and the hat he had bought her, she tried to wish some money—some *blonks,* whatever they were—into his pockets. It was worth a try. If she had succeeded she would never know.

Besides, the image might not be true. Another test?

"Show me the banquet hall of Liliam."

The scene of Stinx faded. And there was the hall, littered with food, water and squabbling gulls. Some of the nobles were sitting on the floor, wringing out their hair and clothes. Veepes ran about, one adorned with tomato. There seemed too much here that was accurate for it to be a trick.

"Well, then," said Tanaquil. She drew in her breath. "Show me—Tanaquil!"

The moment she had said this, she swore. She had not meant that. She had meant Tana*kil*. She did not need, after all, to be shown herself standing here.

But a fresh scene was forming in the sorcerous mirror.

"No. No, I meant—"

Tanaquil broke off.

Clouds melted at the edges of the mirror. The whole of it was tinged with softest blue, then green.

Tanaquil saw . . .

"But that can't—"

It was the guest room in Jaive's fortress. The green walls, the green and gold bed. And on the bed . . .

On the bed.

"Don't play about. Let's try again. Mirror, mirror, on the table. Show me what is real and stable."

The image did not even tremble. It stayed solid now as if it were only the view beyond a window.

On the green and gold bed lay a young woman with long, fiery red hair. She wore a tunic and a divided skirt. She seemed to be asleep. You saw her breathe slowly, in and out, in and out.

On her knees lay a small fur rug. No. A furry peeve. You could not be mistaken. The snout and ears, the paws and tail.

The peeve was asleep, too.

At the side of the bed, Jaive was standing. She was crying. Crying just like a girl of fifteen or a child of four. *Crying*. Big glistening tears.

"Oh, Mother, what is it?"

And then there was Worabex, the grand magician, patting Jaive's shoulder, putting his arm around Jaive. He looked grave and perplexed.

This time, sound came from the mirror. Tanaquil heard his voice. "I'm sorry. I've tried everything I can think of. She's alive. You can see that. But I can't get her back. Even the peeve won't respond. He's her familiar, of course. He'll be with her wherever she is. You must take comfort, my love, from that."

Tears spilled out of Tanaquil's eyes also. She did not know why.

At the foot of the bed sat a smaller blonder peeve, quite still. Was this *Adma*?

And there in the corner, the woolly camel, its forefeet tucked under, lying and looking on with big, old, tolerant eyes.

"Oh," said Tanaquil. She turned from the mirror, at a loss. There beside her sat the peeve, who had come in unheard. The peeve looked at the mirror. "Us." He sounded sure and pleased. Then, sad, *"Us."*

"How can it be us? We're here."

"In," said the peeve.

A door slammed.

The image in the mirror cracked and sheered off like a green-blue-red snow storm. The mirror was blank.

"Blast! *Blast!*" someone shouted outside.

Tanaquil and the peeve oozed invisibly out through the walls.

The princess stood at the center of her pillared room. She was covered in trifle, tomatoes, and seagull droppings.

"I will!" she screamed. "I couldn't but I will. For Jharn—for me—I'll do it tomorrow. Worraday. At the vyger hunt!"

XIV

In the morning, it was Worraday. (Worry-Day?)
Tanaquil had not slept. She had not wanted to, or felt she could.

She had stood some while near the bed of the princess, watching *her* sleep. Asleep, Tanakil looked just like Tanaquil asleep in the magic mirror.

But the mirror, it seemed, had shown a false image after all. Tanaquil and the peeve could not be both there and here. Anyway, how had the camel got upstairs to the guest room? Had Jaive really been crying? Had Worabex, powerful and a know-all, lost his sorcerous knack and not been able to help?

She dismissed it. There were other things to think about.

As Princess Tanakil slept, the veepe crawled into her arms. The peeve, apparently no longer in a fighting mood, left it alone.

Tanakil, perhaps dreaming, said to the veepe, "I should have. I *meant* to. I could have poisoned the tomatoes, and that wine at the race. Why didn't I? She'd be dead by now. I'd be Sulkana. I'd marry Jharn."

So Tanakil really had not tried to murder Lili yet. All the mad confusion, after the race and at the feast, had been quite unnecessary. What else?

Tanaquil had been determined to talk to the princess. In the end she had not been able to think what to say. What *could* you say to your other self?

But I have to do something.

In her dreams, the princess was muttering about potent ancient herbs that killed.

Finally, Tanaquil, still invisible, and the invisible peeve, went floating off through the walls of Hoam-Harm, and up to the calm of the roof garden.

Some birds were singing beautifully to the sinking Rose of stars. In the east—it probably was the east—the red morning sun was rising. The sky washed through black to dark turquoise to apple green.

Where is this place? The animals are weird and crazy. It's lovely with colors. They don't eat meat or fish here, yet they're going on a vyger hunt. What is a vyger?

On a flight of steps among some ornamental yews, someone was singing badly to a badly played lute.

"Her eyes, sweet as a sheep's . . ."

Oynt?

Tanaquil drifted invisibly near.

There he sat on the steps by a large pot full of geraniums. He wore a nasty yellow color that clashed with everything all by itself. His little fat face was full of hopeless sorrow.

"Oh, Lady Feather,

We should be together!
But you vanished away
Like a needle in hay!"

Tanaquil grimaced. Even the geraniums looked fed up. But Oynt was now one more lost lover. In a way it was a nuisance. If Tanaquil put on her disguise as Lady Feather, Oynt would tell her what a vyger was.

Oynt put aside the lute upon some words about sailing down a river with a zither, to seas green as peas.

"If she'd been here, I could have told her about vygers. I'm sure they don't have vygers in Umbrella."

Tanaquil invisibly blinked. Had she made him say this?

Oynt continued aloud to the apparently empty air.

"How the vygers are green, with stripes, and huge green eyes. How they hunt in packs. They mark their tree, and creep up on it. They leap as one, and eat all its leaves. So after the attack it stands bare, as in winter." Oynt raised mournful eyes. "Just like my heart.

"Oh, (tinkle-squeak went the lute) Lady Feather,
You stripped my heart like a vyger,
Of all its leaves of love!"

The peeve made a gesture of putting his paw down his throat in order to throw up.

Really, the peeve was now far too human. Adma would probably have cured him. But would he ever see Adma again?

"I suppose, if they're all going on this hunt, we'd better go too," she said to the peeve, among the shrubbery.

Two young girls passed along the path.

One said to the other, "I heard someone speak in that bush!"

"Yes. Don't look. There's wild magic about. Some man in a village found a pocketful of blonks. Seventeen and a half people have seen a red unicorn."

Tanaquil stared after them.

So she *had* been able to repay Stinx. But as before, did the unicorn hold the key to all this madness?

I like order. That's why I mend things.

A little voice seemed to answer Tanaquil in her head, "And that's why you always end up living in chaos. So you can put it right."

If life is a race of rotted chairs, I have to mend *them?*

Indeed everyone seemed to go on the hunt, except for Oynt. He was in disgrace, having only just told the Princess Tanakil, who anyway, in her rage and mix up, had forgotten, that the spy-assassin-sorceress had escaped the dungeon.

Tanaquil had witnessed this scene, the princess screaming and Oynt cowering, through a window.

"She could be anywhere!"

"Yes, madam. I'm sorry, madam. There's wild magic. She was probably only part of that. Some demon. I met a demon, too, madam. It took the form of a wonderful woman. But she's vanished away like a—"

"Get *out!*"

Tanaquil was reminded of her thoughts about the camel getting upstairs in her mother's fortress, because the court of the Sulkana rode out for the hunt down a broad stairway that ran to the beach. And their mounts were some large creatures, softly dappled fawn, with very long necks. Guafs, they were called. They seemed placid, not even bothered by the roar of the waterfall. They stepped with care down all the steps, their peculiar built-up saddles creaking. Tanaquil floated after.

Crowds were on the beach beside the sea, which might have been said to be green as peas, perhaps.

Everyone cheered. The people cheered the court and the court cheered the people.

"Do they have to do something different here every day?" Tanaquil, unthinking, asked aloud.

"Oh, yes," replied a young man on a guaf. "It's the tradition at Tablonkish." Then he turned to his neighbour and added, "Did you say that?"

"I said, who were you talking to."

They glared at each other, and the procession of great gliding, swaying guafs went on, along the pale green beach, where gulls were flying over, or swimming in and under the water. Then up through pastures of scarlet poppies, and inland, back to the forest-jungle.

Riding through the forest, musicians played, and people sang, so maybe leaving Oynt behind had been the best idea.

The trees were richly green, and in places grapes hung from wild vines. The red flowers twined with orange flowers. Birds made their own music, or hooted, and sometimes mysterious bluish forms, which might have been some sort of monkey, swung over, and flowers, white this time, fluttered down from far up in the forest canopy.

There was no sign of and no word spoken of the savage vygers that attacked trees. But there had been a little more said of them at the start. It seemed they were capable of tearing you limb from limb, and so the hunt was quite chancy.

Tanaquil wondered if the hunt intended to kill the vygers. There were large baskets slung on some of the guafs. Perhaps they were full of bows, spears, axes, and knives.

Personally, Tanaquil disliked hunts. She had been taken on one during her travels about her own world. The prince of that region was a very keen huntsman. Tanaquil knew that many people needed to eat meat, and had no quarrel with that. But the preposterous view that killing something, often quite carelessly, messily, and cruelly, was a *sport* had caused her to dislike the jolly and condescending prince, said by everyone else to be noble and good-hearted. (She had already been disappointed in his princess. Everyone had also said she was elegant, lovely, and concerned with the well-being of the kingdom. But Tanaquil found her showily but badly dressed, self-obsessed, and tiresome.) When the prince offered to teach Tanaquil how to pot birds, "a fine day out, she must not be so silly and squeamish," she gave him such a loud lecture comparing the size of his nose and ears with that of his brain, a personal thing she would normally never have mentioned, that she was asked to leave the kingdom before sundown.

Somehow, though, this hunt did not have the same feel.

Near noon—the warm sun was high in the forest—the court party rode into a clearing.

Another waterfall, much smaller but just as busy as the one in Tablonkish, plashed into a dark green pool. The flowers grew so thickly here that they were like a carpet.

Across the pool was a marvellous, insane house made,

so it looked, from fallen trees, which had grown back into the ground and started new trees, which in their turn added to the house. Between the green and black of the trunks and boughs were crimson and white stained glass windows, and mobiles of golden stars hung clinketing delicately in the breeze.

Tanaquil, floating unseen in the air among the riders, had become quite bold. She whispered in the pearl-hung ear of Velvet, "Where's this?"

"The hut of Fnim," said Velvet, "son of Phnom."

"I know, darling," said Rorlwae.

"Know what?" said Velvet.

Birds flew up from Fnim's hut roof. They circled over, and went back among the trees and glass.

There was a door of black wood, which now opened. A black pig came out, walking on its hind legs and leaning on a staff. It wore a helmet.

"Password," said the pig.

The whole court took a breath and shouted: "Ook, said the bad goose."

The pig stood stolidly.

"Wrong. That was last month."

There was laughter and exclamation, and Fnim came out, and patted the pig, which got back on four legs.

Fnim's clown's face was all smiles. He had excellent, clear gray eyes.

"He's only joking. What's a password? Come in and dine."

The noon dinner was informal. They sat about a huge room with walls and roof of trees, and hung with stars and colored silks. They sat on benches, chairs, rugs on the floor. The pig and Fnim waited on them, bringing dishes of white cheese and nuts, green onions, berries, hot loaves, iced cakes, grapes, plums and apples, and bottles of wine. Not one plate or glass in Fnim's hut was the same as another, but all were beautiful, of strange patterns, shapes, tints.

Sunlight trickled through in sprinkles of gold, and probably if rain fell, it would do the same. There were stacks of rainshades in every corner.

Fnim finally sat down with the Sulkana and Jharn. Tanakil sat alone, at some distance.

There had been a small mishap on the way, the only one. Something in a saddlebag Tanakil had been fiddling with had blown up suddenly, turning half her dress, and all of the veepe, bright emerald. Now both of them sulked. Her face was squashed down in awful lines.

Jharn and Lili began by being very formal. But then Fnim kept making them laugh. Fnim made everyone laugh, including invisible Tanaquil. The peeve showed signs of wanting to appear to Fnim. Tanaquil restrained the peeve.

The black pig had been joined by a pink pig. They were brewing tea in a large cauldron at the central hearth. Neither talked now, and Tanaquil wondered if the black pig had only been trained to grunt in a particular way that sounded like words.

Studying Fnim, Tanaquil saw he entertained less by telling jokes, than by the way he carried on. His face seemed made of rubber. Once he turned, without warning, a flawless somersault. Lili clasped her hands. For a moment she looked about ten years old.

Outside, the long-necked guafs browsed.

"Oh—one's eating your roof, Fnim."

"It can do with a prune."

"The guaf?"

"The roof."

"Unless we give the guaf some prunes," said Lili. She looked surprised at her quip. Fnim smiled at her. She said, "Will you come with us on the hunt, Fnim?" Her pale face had flushed as if with her own smile. Perhaps she had caught the sun.

"Why not?" said Fnim. "I'll bet you, Lili, I can take three vygers."

Tanaquil frowned. The peeve, watching her, frowned.

In her corner, Tanakil, frowning, was tearing a green edge off her half-green gown, and stuffing it into a small flask.

Then putting her silver-ringed finger over the top of the flask, she seemed to be letting something drip inside.

The hunt did not go out again until the sun was westering over the forest. This was the right time, apparently, for vygers.

Tanaquil kept near her double. In the end, she was sitting behind the princess on her guaf, and the peeve was creeping invisibly round and round the green veepe, blowing on it or snickering in its ears.

After the veepe had jumped in the air and fallen off the guaf ten times, it bolted away, jumping instead into one of the weapons baskets slung over another animal. Rummaging, it disappeared under the basket's cover. Princess Tanakil, her frown now set in stone, seemed not to see it had gone.

Tanakil's eyes were fixed only on Lili. The Sulkana rode between Fnim and Jharn. Velvet and Rorlwae were just behind. They were all laughing and singing and telling silly stories, yes, even the Sulkana. Even the spare guaf, given Fnim to ride, looked pleased.

Everyone seemed to be pleased, in fact, except for Tanakil.

Her eyes look red like her hair. At last now, her eyes are truly full of murder.

Yet, if Tanakil had been making her poison as they rode, and in the hut, she had done it in front of them all. Did she want to be seen?

The forest was darkening, purpling, as the sun moved. There began to be a lot of clearings, and here and there a growing tree stood bare. This was sinister, the shadows gathering, the leafless summer trees. Evidently, they were in the place of the vygers.

Rorlwae held up his arm.

At once, everyone reined in their guafs. Silence fell.

No birds were singing, not in this part of the forest. No monkeys swung over. Not even a single butterfly played.

An ominous low rumble began.

The hair rose on Tanaquil's invisible scalp. She gripped the peeve, whose tail she alone could see was bushy as a chimney brush.

Then through the trees, through the shadows, they came. A huge slinking pack. Great ghostly green cats, striped and barred with black, their eyes like burning lamps. They were all purring. This purr was one of the most frightening sounds Tanaquil thought she had ever heard.

Then came the slam of basket lids, the rush of dropped coverings. The weapons were coming out—

Tanaquil ducked with an oath as a hail, a storm of huge green missiles, went roaring over her head.

They bounced down among the vygers: Cabbages; lettuces; cauliflowers; marrows; spinach.

And the vygers were growling now, pouncing and rending, tearing up the vegetables, stuffing their vicious and whiskery faces green into green.

Brave, mad Fnim was off his guaf. He was running forward. A huge vyger tore towards him and he threw a lettuce neatly into its jaws.

Cries of acclaim. "Brilliantly done, Fnim!"

"Better even than Phnom!"

Everyone was dismounting, running in among the deadly vygers, stuffing their muzzles with vegetables.

Tanaquil laughed. She hugged the peeve weakly. "I see—do you see? If they feed them, it lessens the damage to the trees. Oh, peeve, what a world."

Jharn was there, pushing a head of broccoli between a vyger's grinning teeth.

The enormous yellow claws were padding with pleasure now. The vygers purred in menace, growled when happy.

And there, there in the trees, that flame of red—what was it? A fire, the setting sun?

The red unicorn flickered through the clearing and was gone.

It was at this instant that someone, probably by mistake, of all the green things in the baskets, threw Tanakil's dyed veepe to the vygers.

The veepe flew through the air, chops full of lettuce, and dropped towards the center of the thrashing pandemonium.

A vyger raised its awful head and opened wide its jaws—

Tanaquil, numb with panic, glimpsed the face of the princess. She had not even seen.

The veepe missed the fangs of the vyger. It seized the marrow the vyger had been about to eat.

"No—" shouted Tanaquil.

Vyger and veepe had each one end of the marrow, and the vyger's eyes seared with wrath.

From somewhere the peeve sprang. It had got free of Tanaquil, and become visible. People pointed it out. "Is that yours?" "No, I think it's Irk's."

The peeve fell on the vyger's neck and sank in its teeth.

"Foul! Foul!" yelled the court.

The vyger spun, purring, eyes inflamed. The veepe got its tail, the peeve kicked its nose.

They were in a heap now, brown and two unmatched greens. Flailing, honking, yowling, *purring*—all those *teeth*.

It was Jharn, then Rorlwae, who ran forward, pushed the marrow into the vyger's jaws and hauled off the peeve and veepe. Fnim rolled the vyger over, gave it a smacking kiss. The vyger struggled up, and went loping off.

All the vygers were running away. They made little whimpering noises.

In disbelieving relieved disgust, Tanaquil slid down

from the guaf and took the newly escaping peeve in her arms.

"That was *clever.* I think. Well done, I think. But go invisible again, quickly. Do those things lose their ferocity when they've been fed?"

She looked. The vygers were gone. All comedy was gone.

How dark the forest was. How dark. The sun must have sunk. Above the clearing, only a smoky red, shining dully on the remains of cabbages and bits of leeks.

Almost everybody was separated in groups. The veepe was being fed a lettuce by Velvet. There were Jharn and Rorlwae and Fnim, comparing veepe and peeve bites and vyger bruises. In the turf the paw marks of the vygers, redly-edged from sunfall as if with blood.

And Lili, Sulkana Liliam, over there, over there at the clearing's rim, looking to where the vygers had fled.

How dark. How dark the forest is. Nothing funny anymore.

And there is Princess Tanakil, my double, my other self, prowling through the clearing all alone. Veepe forgotten, Jharn forgotten, everything forgotten, with that flask in her hand.

Tanaquil, somehow having to walk, her invisible legs made of lead, went after. She could not hurry. It was like an evil dream. She must have put down the peeve.

"You must be thirsty," said Tanakil to her sister that she hated, her sister who was going to marry and keep Tanakil's only love.

"Perhaps I am, a little. What is it?"

"Just that herb tea you like."

"Thank you, Tantal."

She too, she too used the pet name. Lili-Liliam. *Tantal.*

What was it from? Tantalizing, or from childhood, Tanakil a little taller than Liliam—Tan-tall . . .

How dark the forest.

Red all smeared from the sky. The light of star-rise. The Rose rising. Rising upon this scene of death.

The flask. She had mixed something in it, something terrible. This time she really had. You need only look at the face of Tanakil to *know*.

She watched as her sister Liliam raised the flask to her lips.

And unseen, Tanaquil stood, frozen as the depths of winter, stripped more bare than any tree of its life. *Cold.*

Soon Liliam would be colder.

"Stop!" screamed Tanaquil. She had two voices. How?

Because Tanakil had screamed it too.

In a flapping lunge, she had knocked the flask from Liliam's hand. The mixture, black in the dark, steamed stickily on Liliam's once perfect dress.

"What? Why did you—?"

"It wouldn't be good for you."

"Oh, Tantal, really."

"No. I mixed it up. Something that exploded, and a herb, in my ring—"

"Wasn't that rather complicated, just to make tea?"

"You don't—you don't—understand. I'll tell you, I have to—"

"Oh," said Liliam. Her face had gone utterly white. It gleamed like silver. "Oh, look. And I never thought they were real."

Tanakil turned wildly.

Tanaquil did the same.

There in the shadow and the starlight stood the red unicorn.

The rest of the court was far away. They had not seen
what happened. They did not see the unicorn now.

But Tanakil, Liliam's sister, almost her murderer, cried:
"It's come to punish me. The sword of the horn. Here I
am. Here!"

And the unicorn turned and galloped away, weightless
as red smoke.

But Tanakil ran after it. All the stone-set of her face was
torn like the cabbages, torn to rags of terror and loss. Her
eyes were like blind windows with a raging fire behind
them.

She ran after the unicorn.

And Tanaquil, almost as blind, as mad, ran after her.

Leaving the Sulkana Liliam standing like a small white
statue, all alone in the darkness.

XV

But in the heart of the forest, it was darker still.

Tanaquil ran. The trees glanced by like black poles against a reddish, low afterglow, or paler against night sky, night leaves.

Ahead, the princess, a sound of snapping twigs, stumbles, and small animals leaping aside.

Far, far ahead, the unicorn, unseen, noiseless.

A phrase droned in Tanaquil's mind, something said once by her mother, "He led her a dance."

She had been puzzled. What did it mean? It meant this.

And then Princess Tanakil, with a shriek, tumbled right over something. She fell with a sound like small bells and crushed paper bags.

There was another clearing. Overhead the dark sky with its choruses of singing silver stars. The Rose not yet high enough to be spotted.

The princess lay sprawled over a small fallen tree trunk. Some aggressive-looking rabbits, which had been feeding, lurked in the clover.

Between two of the farthest trees, the red unicorn stood quite still.

It was now, by night, the red of a dying fire. Brighter than by day, yet more sombre too. The horn, as it turned its head, flicked the starlight in a way Tanaquil remembered.

She needed to be visible. She was.

Tanaquil helped Tanakil to her feet.

"Let go. Thank you. Who are you? Oh, it's—"

"Oh it's me. Sorry."

"*Sorceress*. Is that beast yours?"

"No. Unicorns don't belong to anyone. But I think, however, both of us have something to do with it."

"Don't speak in riddles," snarled Tanakil. She fumbled at her waist, "I'll banish you with a spell, you demon."

"I'm not a demon. And I think you've done enough magic-making for one day. Don't you?"

Tanakil stared at her. Her face was uncreasing. She looked hurt and miserable. "What do you mean?"

"Your sister. Lili-Liliam. The poisoned flask."

"It was a cup of tea."

"It was poison. You almost admitted it to her. You almost let her drink it."

"I should have done. I *should*. She's a witch."

"No she isn't. She's not as clever or sensitive as you are. Jharn loves you, after all, not her. Isn't that bad enough for her? Do you really need to *kill* her too?"

Tanakil began to cry. They were the bitter heavy sobs of one who has not allowed herself to cry very much. Of one who has tried to stop thinking of what she wants, except maybe for five or ten minutes every day.

Tanaquil went over to the princess. With the oddest feeling, she put her arms about her.

"It's all right to cry. Go on. Poor old Tantal."

She held Tanakil close and Tanakil wept into Tanaquil's almost identical unicorn-red hair.

Across the clearing, the unicorn, silent, immobile, seemed to watch.

"The best thing is, you didn't do it. You stopped her drinking it. I mean—darn Liliam. You were the one who would have had to live with killing her."

"She'll know now. She'll have them behead me."

"No, she won't. She's too slow to realize what you did. All she saw anyway was the unicorn. And then you chased after it. And she was too grown-up and proud to do that."

"The unicorn is here to stab me," said Tanakil stubbornly, straightening up and wiping her eyes on her sleeves. "I'm ready."

"I don't . . . think so. Anyway. It's my unicorn too."

"You said—"

"You and I," said Tanaquil. She took a breath and said firmly, "We're the same, you know. You're me, I'm you."

"*You're* an apparition, a demon."

"Hush," said Tanaquil gently.

Across the glade, the unicorn was approaching now, picking its fragile, starlit way, and as it passed, the grasses seemed to catch soft fire, but the rabbits fed peacefully beneath its hoofs, and it stepped delicately over them.

"Quill," said Tanakil, using the name Tanaquil had offered before, "what does it want?"

"I don't know. I expect it'll show us."

Tanakil said, in a rush, "I should have been Sulkana. I'm

one year older than Lili. But my mother ran away from Tandor, our horrible father. And she ran away from me. Lili's mother stayed until she died."

"Parents can be awful pests," said Tanaquil.

The unicorn was only a foot or so from them.

Slowly it turned. Its side was now towards them.

"What . . . what is it?" whispered Tanakil.

"I think . . . but it wouldn't—"

"Here, me," cried a voice, raucous and breathless. Then another similar voice, "Me! Me! Here!"

The princess and Tanaquil spun round.

The peeve came thumping into the glade, as if fired from a bow, the dyed-green veepe, a lettuce leaf still caught in its jaws, darting after.

The outraged rabbits spat and fled.

"Me!" "Me!"

"All right, it's you two. Now be quiet," said Tanaquil.

"Go unicorn," said the peeve. *"Rides."*

Tanaquil glanced at the unicorn again. It stood, patient, timeless. It was smaller than the black unicorn had been, yet strong. It would be easy, to swing up on its back.

But you could not ride a unicorn.

She thought of the Perfect World. There they had not even ridden their horses.

And yet, was this the gesture of its friendship? It would take them somewhere. And it would carry them, the way you might carry a tired child.

Tanaquil went to the unicorn, and put her hand, stilly, on its neck. It felt of warm satin, it smelled of grass, and night. It was solid. It waited.

"Is it a fact we get up on your back?"

After all, why else had she thought of it? Why else had the *peeve* thought of it?

"Come on, Tantal," she said to Tanakil.

"What?"

"This." Tanaquil, used to the problems of horses and camels, propelled herself up with no trouble. "Sit behind me."

"On a unicorn? That would be unlawful."

"Trust me."

"Trust *you!*"

"Who else," said Tanaquil, "*can* you trust?"

She saw the starlight gleam in the round eyes of peeve and veepe, watching and panting. Then Tanakil had jumbled up untidily behind her, cursing, slipping. The unicorn kept steady as a rock.

"Are you on?"

"Yes—ah! Now I am."

And now what?

Tanaquil was not really prepared. Tanakil was certainly not prepared.

The unicorn jumped. It jumped straight off the ground into the air. And hung there. Then it sprang round the glade, its feet galloping over nothing, its head towards the sky.

Tanakil gave a muffled squall.

"It's all right. We have to trust it."

"Trust you, trust *it*—"

The unicorn swam on for another swift circuit; it was flying, but without wings.

Fifteen feet below, peeve and veepe stared up.

And then something quite idiotic, quite beautiful. From the back of the peeve two pale brown feathery wings sprouted. He too lifted up into a flight. Hardly graceful, but lively, he bowled around the glade, paws pummelling, making gratified *spuff-spuffs*.

At this the unicorn rose upward, ten feet, twenty, directly towards the sky above the glade.

Tanakil uttered her best curse yet.

"Hold tight. Yes, you *are,* aren't you," choked Tanaquil as Tanakil almost strangled her with one clutching arm and squeezed her breathless round the middle with the other.

The peeve came whizzing by, reversed, and capered round them. "Nice! Nice!"

Perhaps they could all have flown up this high anyway. Did the peeve even need wings?

The unicorn hung over the treetops now. The peeve, diverted, rooted in a nest with his snout, and a large bird popped up and pecked him.

On the ground, the veepe looked with yearning eyes. Tanaquil could hear it whining, poor thing.

The peeve batted the irritated bird into its nest, and shot back towards the ground. Just above the veepe, the peeve lashed out with his tail.

With no sensible thought left in her mind at all, Tanaquil saw two black wings sprout in turn from the veepe's dyed body. It too plunged up into the air.

But the unicorn was cantering, wingless, into the highest black cup of the night.

She clung to it, and Tanakil clung mercilessly to her, and

behind came the two daft flying, and decidedly paddling, forms of the veepe and the peeve, their four eyes brighter than the stars. While the lettuce leaf fluttered in the veepe's jaws like a flag.

XVI

They went so high, they caught up with the last of the sunset. It reappeared below them all along the hem of the world.

But the scarlet sunset had made the shape of a red unicorn, with a star for an eye. And the clustered stars of the Rose made up its horn, the final coil and curl ending in the dark upper sky.

The unicorn on which they rode veered smartly. It rushed now like a wind, straight for the Rose.

Tanakil went "Oh-oh." She burrowed into Tanaquil's back.

Tanaquil held fast to the mane and neck of the magical beast. She had relaxed, for surely, after all, this was a dream. She would be shaken off and fall and wake with a bump, in bed. But where would the bed be? Domba's house? The magnolia tree? Or the guest room in Jaive's fortress?

The glow of the stars of the Rose was growing brighter

and more bright. In a few minutes it seemed as bright as a clear bluish-rosy dawn.

Transparent bubble clouds went by beneath, like pretty paperweights that were weightless.

"Tantal—if I'm not dreaming you, or if you're not dreaming me—you *must* look! It's first class."

Tanakil stirred.

"We're so high now, we're flying into the stars."

"No, that's impossible," said Tanaquil.

But it was not impossible.

Tanaquil knew, from her mother's early lessons, that all stars were suns, huge balls of flame and gas, millions of miles from any world. But here, in this curious place, it seemed the stars of the Rose at least were like the stars she had imagined as a little girl.

And now the unicorn sailed among them.

Far more than could be counted from below, they hung, trembling slowly, sparkling and spangling, some as great as the palace of Hoam-Harm, some even larger, some the same size as Tanaquil herself. And there were others, small as apples, as cherries, but all revolving, burning bright. Their glassy silveryness was washed with pale sapphire and jade, with specks of flame and soft dazzles of lightning. They were like giant opals, like diamonds. And yet, they were stars, stars as stars should be, with no reason to them, no science, no logical, down-to-earth answer.

They rang and sang too, faintly. On their own. And when the tail of the unicorn brushed the little ones, they gave off little notes and chimes, and sometimes even a sound like a child's laughter.

"It's amazing."

"Yes. It is."

Behind them, the peeve and the veepe came flapping through, now and then pausing to roll over in the air and strike a star with a paw. Tanaquil was glad to see this seemed to cause no damage.

Of course, the stars were tough as steel, perhaps indestructible. They were *stars,* for heaven's sake.

In the center of the Rose cluster, or perhaps it was not the center, but it seemed to be, there was a plain like a smoky mirror, stretching, horizontally, through the jewelry of lights.

Nothing was on this plain, which had bevelled edges like a mirror, until the unicorn sank down, and landed there.

A moment after they touched down, a tinsel gush started from above. A waterfall of stars, or the embers of stars, was falling to the plain.

It seemed time to dismount. They did so, and stood under this heavenly downpour.

"Where have we come to, Quill?"

"I don't know, Tantal. But it looks all right."

"And why?"

Tanaquil drew her eyes from all the hypnotizing loveliness and stared hard at the only recognizable things. Peeve and veepe were playing noisily in the star shower. Tanakil stood with her half-green dress. She no longer looked cruel, or wretched. Her face had been washed clean.

"I think," said Tanaquil, measuring out her words, "we had to come away from the world. *Leave the world behind.* And then be face to face."

"We're doubles."

"We're the same."

"So then?" said Tanakil.

The crystalline shower seemed glittering in Tanaquil's mind. Her mind, like the face of her other self, was being rinsed clear. Crystal clear.

"Listen. It's so simple. Sit down."

They sat close, legs crossed, leaning towards each other, while the veepe and the peeve rolled over and over in sprays of unearthly gems.

"Honj—I mean Jharn—loves you," said Tanaquil. "You love him. That's really all you both care about. So blast the rest of it. Let Lili be Sulkana. Let her throw you both out. Tell him to leave her, and you go with him. What does the rest matter?"

"No, that's too simple."

"Why shouldn't it be simple?"

"But she," said Tanakil in a rough little voice, "what about Lili?"

"Look, if he doesn't love her, he'll feel bad, and he'll probably make her feel bad. He's no use to her. He wants to be with you. She's so honorable, she'll have to agree. And oh, Tantal, don't you *see*? If he leaves her, then she's free to love someone else. And she does, Tantal, though none of you know it. She loves Fnim."

"But he's too *old*!"

"She wants someone to replace her father. To give her the father she never had. Not awful cold demanding Zorander—I mean Tandor—but a kind, happy, carefree, funny father. Someone who can make her laugh. Make her tell jokes. Make her feel more woman, not a piece of chilly stone. And someone who needs her too, to calm him down. And you, my girl," said Tanaquil fiercely, "need someone to stop you breaking things and blowing things up."

Tanakil shook her head. Nodded her head.

A peculiar shiver went over her dress. The green half vanished. The stain was gone. While under the waterfall of stars, the veepe was black and had stardust, not lettuce in its mouth.

"If it's so easy, shouldn't we go back and do it? If so, *how* do we go back on our own?"

"The unicorn," said Tanaquil. She turned and gazed about for it. The unicorn was not there. "Wait. I think I see. I think—Tantal, the unicorn—it's a part of you, of me. It's . . . do you know this expression, the Heart's Desire?"

"I know the expression," said Tanakil, "but *how do we get down from here?*"

Tanaquil got up.

"You and I, again. Sorceress. And so this, it's like everything else. It's actually embarrassingly simple."

When Tanaquil, holding firmly to Tanakil's hand, jumped off the edge of the glass plain, Tanakil screeched. But the stars only chimed, and then they were floating serenely down through the showers of the stars, through the jewelry work of the Rose, with the peeve and the veepe paddling after them, obedient for once. Only the piece of lettuce must have been dropped somewhere in the sky. Would it too become enchanted?

"It's silly," nagged Tanakil. "Everything can't be as straightforward as this—"

"Perhaps it is. Perhaps everything always is. Even the terrible things. Even the heartbreaking things. Perhaps the answer is there and it's so simple we never see it."

They flowed down through the clouds, which had a smell of rain and lightning. Their hair streamed cool. They laughed.

The sky was darkening, then the sky was black and the stars far off.

Veepe and peeve, like two badly-designed birds, wrestled in thin air, dropped half a mile, were seen below, scurrying and fluttering over the tops of the forest.

"Go to him at once," said Tanaquil. "To Jharn. And to Lili."

"There'll be a three-hour-long row."

"Better than a lifelong absolute foulness."

Beyond the forest, lights were dimly to be seen.

"There's Sweetish. And there's Tweetish, and Tablonkish. And there, I think that could even be the town of Kohm Pleetish."

Tanaquil sighed, and tilting her head, looked back at the Rose. A tiny green brilliant had appeared. No doubt she had just not seen it before. Either that, or the dropped lettuce leaf had turned into a star.

On the forest floor, while woken birds fussed and bustled in the branches above, Tanaquil and Tanakil shyly, bossily, shook hands.

The peeve and the veepe washed each other, then had a quick fight for old time's sake.

"Good luck, Tantal."

"Good luck, Quill."

They began to hear calls, and to see the flash of torches through the trees.

"A search party for me," said Tanakil. "Useless fools—"

"You don't need to be angry now. Go straight to him."

"Yes. To him." Tanakil smiled, which suited her.

As the princess walked away through the aisles of the night wood, sometimes throwing a stick for her veepe, (which still had wings) Tanaquil felt, as if for the first, the rhythm of her own pulses.

What Tanakil must do, she, Tanaquil, must do also.

Even so, she watched until, some while after her double had disappeared, there came glad shouts of finding, and a trumpet call.

"Now for their three-hour row," said Tanaquil. "But we, we go home." The peeve looked at her expectantly. "Am I right?" she asked him. "That's simple, too?"

"In," said the peeve. *"Out."*

"I thought so."

Tanaquil bent and picked him up. He was as warm as toast, as known as her own self. Honj was still a stranger. To love was not to know. That had still to be learned. It might take all the years of her life. How wonderful.

"Hold tight." The peeve, still obedient, stuck every single tooth and claw into her clothes and arms. *"Ouch!"* Here we go. Up and *out!"*

It was like surfacing from a deep and swirling river. All things, cold and hot, molten and impassable, running, spilled the other way. They pushed, like two needles, through a thick black cloth, through and through, and shoved their heads, their bodies, minds and hearts and souls, out into a dark, and to a golden light.

Three

XVII

Tanaquil sat on a bench, her chin on her hand, gazing down the long walk where the cypresses lushly grew, to the great gleaming pond. Already ducks had flown in and found it. And sometimes, in the dusk, a wandering jackal might come there to drink, or a band of dusty peeves. The garden was overgrown, being too big for Jaive and Worabex to look after on their own. In the cold nights, the flowers had not lasted. The walk was thick with weeds. Soon it would be only an ornate oasis. But for all that, it had brought greenery and water to the desert.

Jaive meant well. She always did.

"And look, Mother, there's a cactus. That's come up on its own."

"Yes, dear. I don't mind. I'm only glad you're here."

"Thank you, Mother. It's been lovely. But remember, to-morrow. . ."

"Tomorrow you're leaving me again." Jaive sounded disapproving. Tanaquil realized this was a mask for concern.

"Not for ever. I explained. I have to do what I told

Tanakil to do. I have to find Honj again, with Lizra's army."
She paused in thought. She said, "It will be winter there,
now." Then she said, "I've left it a long time. And after what
Worabex told me—well. I know it's possible Honj has
changed his mind. Lizra would have made him Prince
Consort, even emperor. It's a lot to give up."

"Yes," said Jaive. Her eyes were dull for a moment. Of
course, someone had left *her* to go and be the ruler of a
kingdom.

"Anyway, I have to try. I made a mistake. I should have
stood up for myself, for us both. He may well say no, but
if I don't ask him, I shall never find out. And I'll have to
explain to Lizra, too." Lizra, snow queen in a landscape of
snow. A three-hour row would be nothing to what Lizra
might, probably in utter silence, put on Honj and
Tanaquil.

The light shifted in Jaive's desert garden. Above, that
deep blue sky.

This had been the strangest thing, the oddness of a
blue sky after the green sky over Tablonkish.

Dark, then light: golden. Cobalt.

As she had opened her eyes, lying on the bed, Tanaquil
had felt heavy and immovable. But she moved anyway, and
so found some of the heaviness was the peeve spread on
her legs. But next second the peeve rolled over, and also
sat up blinking.

"Back," said the peeve.

Then there was something like a ball of furry fireworks,
which came shooting from a corner, and Adma the peevess
had landed on the peeve, washing and washing him, kissing his eyes, rubbing his nose with hers. And the peeve,

stupid and soppy beyond all stupid soppiness, flopped over and was allowing all this, with small encouraging squeaks. Adma squeaked too.

And who is here to squeak at me? thought Tanaquil, resentfully and giddily sitting up and getting out of peeveway. Certainly the camel was not here. Nor was Jaive standing crying, or Worabex, infuriatingly fatherly. Something was there, however, on the floor beyond the bed.

It was a thing with two heads, elephant ears, elephant-trunk arms, frog eyes. It was sunk to its enormous stomach in the guest room rug. The room was now freezing cold.

"Salutations," said Epbal Enrax, the cold demon, in its bone-rattling murmur. But a mauvish vapor trailed over it. This indicated it was pleased. *"I will fetch she who is your mother."*

It wobbled like a jelly down through the floor.

Five minutes later, after Tanaquil had washed her face and was brushing her hair, and the peeve and Adma were playing quite violently on the bed, running rippingly up the curtains, biting each other's tails and so on, the door opened and Jaive and Worabex burst in like an unkempt embroidered wave.

"Oh, darling—Oh, Tanaquil—Oh!"

"Hallo, Mother."

But Jaive, for the first time since Tanaquil's childhood, seized Tanaquil in her arms. Jaive hugged her daughter, kissed her, squeezed her; yes, it was Adma all over again.

She loves me, thought Tanaquil. *She really does.*

A little cautiously, she hugged Jaive back.

When at last they separated, Jaive wiped her eyes on one

of her purple kittens, which was clinging to her sleeve. Neither of them seemed to notice. Epbal Enrax had reappeared, holding the other kitten. Probably he liked their color.

"How long," said Tanaquil, "was I—"

"Darling girl. Several weeks. We could do nothing. Nothing!"

Worabex cleared his throat and spoke from the doorway. "Our demons rebelled." Tanaquil recalled the sickly sugar-pink apparitions with charming deer or cat faces and nice manners.

"I can see why. What did they really look like?"

"One doesn't ask. Aside from that, only Epbal Enrax remained loyal. Your glamorous old nurse is knitting him a purple tunic as a reward."

Epbal Enrax put the kitten on to his fat coiled tail. The kitten padded about and curled up, seeming not to be put off by the cold of the demon's person.

"It was the female peeve over there, who found you," said Worabex. "After the waterspout. She ran up here. Told your peeve. When we brought you in, your peeve went to join you. A familiar should do that, of course, and be able to. Following this, beyond a spell or two to look after you while you were unconscious, there wasn't much to be done. You're very powerful with your magic, Tanaquil. Do you understand that now?"

"I was in another world," said Tanaquil. "But not physically. Which explains what I could do there. And yet, it was as real as here. As for the peeve, he must somehow have projected his awareness—"

Worabex said, "The mathematics are difficult."

She thought, delighted, *He doesn't properly understand either.*

"We must have a feast, now you're here," cried Jaive, forgetting servants and demons had left.

"Could I just have about six cups of tea?" Tanaquil had asked thirstily.

"Even one cup of tea," said Worabex, "may be a problem."

She found she did not mind them so much now, her mother and romantic Worabex. Love was magical, ludicrous, and everywhere. She remembered their concern for her, seen in the sorcerous mirror. Presumably that had been true, even if the camel was not present.

She told them a little of the other world, and her conclusions. Not much. They did not seem, besides, to want to ask her a great deal. They looked awkward. It was personal.

Finally, over the makeshift meal of biscuits, rolls and porridge—all cold, all hard—that Epbal Enrax had managed to gather, she said to them, "The place I went to was inside me, in my head, wasn't it?"

"Yes," said Jaive. "One of the Inner Worlds."

"There's more than one?"

"As many as are necessary," said Worabex. She sensed he was trying not to sound lofty. There was a mousp sipping from his cup of cold, luckily not hard, tea. Tanaquil regarded it. "Oh. Yes," said Worabex. "I must make my confession. This was the fellow, the stingless one, who went with you before. It wasn't . . . myself."

"You said—"

"I said it to put you off balance. Forgive me. I was so self-conscious, Tanaquil, talking to you on those hills, about visiting your mother. I was trying to get the better of you. I did, however, see you all in the hell world through the *eyes* of the mousp. I'm mage enough for that."

"What about the *flea?*"

Worabex lowered his eyes. "It seemed I was."

"Seemed?"

"An illusion." He straightened up. "I do know about your adventures with Honj. I have to say, I think it was in-evitable that you went into one of the Inner Worlds to find him there."

"It was inevitable because of your experiment with water courses and gardens, which knocked me out!" retaliated Tanaquil.

Jaive wrung her hands. "My dearest—"

"She would have gone anyway," said Worabex. He had decided on loftiness after all. "She is invulnerable. How else did the waterspout effect her?"

Tanaquil, instead of throwing a roll at him, said, "You may be right. But what are they, the Inner Worlds? Dreams?"

"Not at all. Places that might be. Places where we can meet with ourselves."

"But it was *real.*"

"Perhaps," said Jaive softly, "now you've *made* it real."

Tanaquil opened her mouth, closed it.

Worabex said, "What you believe in, can come to be. The basis, of course, of all sorcery."

"I hope it can," said Tanaquil.

Later, again, after the peeves had run off to their nest,

Jaive and Tanaquil walked out into the desert garden. Tanaquil thought about the chattering fluffed-up Adma, and how her own familiar seemed suddenly barely to remember Tanaquil. She was miffed, and also thankful, he needed to get rid of the overhumanness he had accumulated. Then too there had been that little burst of speech from him as they scrambled from the window: "Says nest flies—"

The garden was full of pools, and rivulets, and fountains, that still, despite the flight of the demons, played. (In the fortress, evidence had been left of the rebellion. There were pink sticky messes up and down the walls, burn marks in the floors and stonework. On the stairways the wooden animals and fruits were fighting and wriggling. Now and then howls of rude, disembodied laughter raced down the passages. In the kitchen below, sat a three-foot high, worrying-looking egg. "Epbal Enrax says it's only a giant sparrow," airily explained Jaive.)

"The sun's going down," said Tanaquil. "And then, the moon will rise. There wasn't a moon, there. But some beautiful huge stars they called the Rose."

Jaive took Tanaquil's hand. "Must you go tomorrow? I've neglected you so. Oh, Tanaquil. You're such a powerful sorceress. All these worlds. All these unicorns."

"Mother, you couldn't help neglecting me. It doesn't matter now. You have every right to be happy. So do I. I must go back and talk to Honj."

Jaive dabbed two perfect diamond tears, like two little stars of the Rose. "Yes, dear."

"That Inner World," said Tanaquil. "I'm so sure that somehow it must be real. Somewhere. Although it was quite insane. Wolf-squirrels that thieved nuts. Daffodils, Rot-Chair Races. Did I make it like that so I could deal more easily with my double there?"

Jaive said, "Is any world quite sensible?"

Tanaquil gazed into the sky. Across the garden, about twenty feet up, a strange bulky raft-thing was hovering. Bits of stick protruded from it, and strips of colored cloth hung over. There were glints. Over the edge peered two long snouts. *Says nest flies.* The peeve had stolen Jaive's magic carpet. They had torn it up and added it to the nest. The nest flew.

Tanaquil looked down. She said quickly, "Please go on, Mother. You're helping me."

Jaive said, "Why shouldn't the Inner Worlds be real?" She stood up.

Tanaquil checked the sky. The flying nest was sailing calmly away behind some trees.

"Come with me," said Jaive.

Tanaquil followed Jaive along the cypress walk to the reed-fringed pond.

Jaive made a pass over it.

"My mirrors don't yet work. The demons scribbled on them with sorcerous paint. But this water should do." She spoke old arcane words, and the air parted like ribbons.

"Tanaquil's Inner World," cried Jaive. To Tanaquil grandly she said, "Say whom or what you wish to see."

Tanaquil said, "Show me Princess Tanakil."

At the middle of the pond, a picture slowly formed. It was not very strong, but clear enough.

Tanaquil saw her other self walking hand in hand with Jharn along a street of Tablonkish. They were laughing and swinging their hands, and the veepe, the veepe *flew* ahead of them on its little wings, with a green apple in its mouth.

The picture melted, and a duck splashed down from the bank into the pond. Ripples changed everything into water again.

"Well. She and he are all right. Lili didn't even send them away."

Jaive turned. She said to Tanaquil in a small young voice Tanaquil thought she had never heard before, "You will *write* to me. You will come back, sometimes."

"Yes, Mother. I promise. I want to."

"I've done everything wrongly. Do you forgive me?"

Tanaquil said, "You made me what I am, or you made me make myself. I don't mind being me. Mother, was the camel ever in the guest room?"

"Of course," said Jaive. "I led it there myself, once every day. We tried to put all the things about you that you might know, to help you to get back. It was for that reason too that Worabex sent the message to Honj. Don't be angry."

"No, no, I'm not. It's just, perhaps, perhaps he would have reached here by now. I mean, if he wanted to, he might have ridden very fast. And, well. He hasn't, has he? Worabex sent a letter, by magic too, to Honj, telling him I was lying there, senseless. And Honj doesn't seem to have taken much notice."

"Oh, Tanaquil."

Tanaquil thought, had Jaive ever written, by magic, to Zorander? Had she sat and waited. Waited. Waited.

"Mother, there are a hundred reasons why he might not have been able to come to me. That's why I have to go and find him myself."

XVIII

She talked quite a lot with the camel as they rode. She realized she had got used to talking to the peeve. The camel did not talk back, which was a mixed blessing.

The peeve and Adma had been busy in their nest, found back on the roofs. More of Jaive's jewelry had been stolen for it, a mirror, and a large frying pan Adma was particularly vain of. She liked to sit in it and drum her paws to make it sound.

Tanaquil said nothing about flying. The peeve said nothing about it to her. She told him she would return in a while. She might be alone. She did not know. She might be with Honj. The peeve thumped his tail like a dog at Honj's name. Then forgot Honj and went back to polishing the frying pan for Adma to drum.

Would he forget Tanaquil, too? Surely a witch's familiar, especially one with a flying nest, would never forget his witch? It was good for him, anyway. To be himself. *Most of us need both. Ourselves, and to share with another.*

What am I to do if he has forgotten me?

Honj might be married to Lizra anyway. It might all be too late.

As the desert faded and the fields began, and the cold filled the days as well as the nights, Tanaquil bought a thick cloak and a flask of brandy.

They travelled on and on.

Snow fell, Lizra-like snow, so cold, so pale. But Lizra was not so cold as snow. She had once built a sandcastle. Somehow she had become someone else in Tanaquil's mind, icy little Lili.

They sheltered in barns, in villages, at open hearths on white-lapped hills, when stars also blazed like fires in the sky, and the moon stood on a hilltop.

"That's a fair old horse you've got there," said the ones who had never seen a camel.

Will he remember me? Will he want me? Did he ever want me, or did I only imagine it?

That morning, they took a wrong turn. She had heard by then of the place, a new place, where the great Empress Lizora Veriam had set up her court. There was to be a big winter festival there. It was, they said, in this weather, a three-week journey.

Then, in the snow, the road vanished, they got off into a wood, all bare as if from winter vygers, and ended up at a ruined house, a few stone walls and roof, where, since the wind was blowing up, it seemed wise to have lunch.

Not until she had got down from the camel, and was leading him along the slope to the open door, did

Tanaquil make out some smoke rising from the spot, and smell a fire.

They had better be careful. She had been warned of robbers.

Tanaquil left the camel, and crept forward to the doorway. As she reached it, a figure filled it, swathed in black wool, that let out the glint of a knife.

"Uh, I just be after me sheeps," said Tanaquil, witless, friendly, and ever so poor, to the perhaps-robber in the doorway. Who answered, "Tanaquil."

And coming out into the white daylight, she saw he was Honj.

All thought, all feeling, any warmth, went out of her. She stood there, just what she had pretended, utterly mindless.

"Er, hallo."

"What a greeting. No, 'Fancy meeting you.' No, 'How wonderful to see you.' I should have known better."

She felt herself flush with old familiar rage.

"How did you know anything anyway? I was supposed to be lying unconscious in my mother's fortress."

"Yes, yes. Out of date, sweetheart. That mousp found me again, yesterday. First the dire letter about your accident. Then the cheery news you were up and out and after me."

"Worabex, confound him! How dare he. What do you mean *after* you?"

"Aren't you, then?" he asked. He was so handsome he was ridiculous. Her heart almost choked her. "You don't want me at all. I'm to dissolve in disappointed weeping, here in all this bloody snow."

"Honj—"

"Tanaquil. For God's sake, come inside, and let's freeze by the fire."

In the firelight, all the coppery and blue-steel streams in his dark hair. His eyes steel blue.

She had forgotten *him*. His marvel. His way of moving, of looking at her. He wore the silver ring he had taken from her on his smallest finger. He said he had got someone to make the ring larger. He just sat, holding her hands, which he had first seized, he said, to warm them. While the mulled brandy got cold at their side, and his horse and the camel nibbled ivy off the wall.

"I never was sure," he said, "how you felt. Not really. I thought, 'Yes, she likes me.' Women do like me. But it's nothing much. Not enough to make a demand on me. And Lizra—we were both so shocked by her, weren't we? Guilty. Well, I'd better tell you the whole tale."

She wondered if she could concentrate. She just wanted to sit here for ever, freezing by the fire, holding his hands, looking at him, listening to his voice.

"I tried to make a go of it. I was the perfect gentleman. Lizra was the perfect empress. Everyone was saying I'd be the emperor. But there was such a lot to do. A big ceremonial wedding was the last thing anyone could cope with. Then some king from across the sea sent her word he wanted to make an alliance with her. And he was coming to see to it himself."

"Yes, go on."

"You're distracting me. Is it you, Tanaquil? Is it?"

"It's not me at all. Please say the rest."

"I'll cut it short. Basically the king arrived, and it was

chaos. Morning, noon, night, fanfares, feasts, rituals—
plucking the herring, kissing the cushion—you think I'm
joking? Audiences all day. Spedbo said, and Mukk—"

"Oh, Mukk and Spedbo!"

"Yes. They said, If this was being powerful and rich, they
were off."

"But they didn't *leave* you—"

"No. No, what happened was, one night when we were
all going mad, because this new king insisted on passwords
all over the city and the army, and he had given us this lat-
est one which was, 'I won't be cooked, said the bad
goose.' "

"It was *what*?"

"A gem, wouldn't you say. 'I won't be cooked—' "

"Not *Ook*?"

"Sorry? No, not ook." Honj shook their hands.

"It's just—it's very like—no, never mind."

"Anyway, in the midst of this completely useless idiocy,
Worabex the great magician sent me a mousp. At first
Mukk tried to slice it in half and we all got under the table.
Then Spedbo identified it as our nonsting friend from the
last time. Then he picked it up and it somehow produced,
sorcerously, of course, you'd grasp it, I thought it a bit over
the top: a letter."

"The letter that I was—"

"Had nearly been killed. Were lying near death."

Tanaquil looked down. "That was some weeks ago."

"Yes, Tanaquil. I've been travelling some weeks."

"You mean that—"

"I mean that I sat down, and Spedbo fanned me with
half a loaf from breakfast. And Mukk said if I was going to

throw up, lean that way and avoid the wine bottles. Then I explained. Then they shut up. And I went straight over to Lizra's rooms."

"You . . . did . . ."

"It was just before one of the awful dinners. She was done up in a black dress with sort of silver *claws* all over it. It made me superstitious. But anyway. I said what I must. That I was sorry. But I'd been very wrong. I had to be with you. I *loved* you. I tried to be tactful, but you can't be, saying something like that. I thought you were, I was afraid you'd die. I was cursing myself for letting you go. I thought Lizra would turn into the Ice Queen and have me whipped to death on the spot."

"She didn't."

Honj now lowered his eyes.

"She said, I'll never forget it, she said, 'Oh, Honj, what a burden you've taken from me.' "

"What?"

"She said this password-crazy king—thirty-six if he was a day, old enough to be her father—had proposed he and she get married and unify their kingdoms. And she, she wanted to do just that. She said, and I quote here, 'I've loved you, Honj, but now I have to grow up.' " His eyes flamed with anger, then with laughter.

Tanaquil cried, "Lili and Fnim!"

"So you're insulting me already?"

"No, I'll tell you one day. Oh, Honj. Oh—"

"And so I was loaded with money and presents and terrible things I didn't want, but Spedbo and Mukk grabbed them like kids in a sweet-shop. And as for Waelorr—"

"Wait again. Who?"

"Waelorr. You never met him yet. Good man, tall, black, and handsome. All the girls are after him, but he only likes one called Lace—"

"Not . . . Velvet?"

"Did I say Velvet? I said Lace. Anyhow, those three are with me. Back up the road by a couple of cities. I wanted to get on."

Tanaquil sat away the length of her arms, not letting go his hands. "You're free," she said.

"No," he said. "I'm yours. So it's up to you. Do you want me? Say yes properly this time, or I'll push you in the fire."

"Yes, properly."

And for a moment, in that fire, she saw the shining scarlet shape of the unicorn, bright as a sun. Flying without wings.

"I mean, Tanaquil, I mean I want to marry you, to stay with you. I expect you'll only reply with something sophisticatedly witty, now."

"I'll reply with yes, now," she said. "Is that witty enough?"

He drew her to him. She went to him. The unicorn dimmed. Now it was only in her heart.

He said, in a different voice, "They say love makes the world go round."

Looking at him, it seemed to her that never before had she seen anyone so clearly.

"Then," she said, "we must help to keep it moving."